SUNSET
MANOR

Also by Richard B. Wright

THE WEEKEND MAN
IN THE MIDDLE OF A LIFE
FARTHING'S FORTUNES
FINAL THINGS
THE TEACHER'S DAUGHTER
TOURISTS
ONE JOHN A TOO MANY (FOR CHILDREN)

SUNSET MANOR

RICHARD B. WRIGHT

SEAL BOOKS
McClelland-Bantam, Inc.
Toronto

SUNSET MANOR
A Seal Book / April 1990

Canadian Cataloguing in Publication Data

Wright, Richard B., 1937–
  Sunset manor

ISBN 0-7704-2371-X

I. Title.

PS8595.R57S86   1990   C813'.54   C89-095268-X
PR9199.3.W755S86   1990

COVER PRINTED IN U.S.A.

BG   0 9 8 7 6 5 4 3 2 1

To P _____ again.

An aged man is but a paltry thing,
A tattered coat upon a stick, unless
Soul clap its hands and sing, and louder sing
For every tatter in its mortal dress.

W. B. Yeats

Just a song at twilight
When the lights are low.

Old song

In this novel the institution where events unfold takes its name from the familiar metaphor of the setting sun. The equating of old age with the end of day is a rhetorical commonplace, and those who are charged with the responsibility for attaching names to homes for the elderly have seldom strained after novelty. In the interests of verisimilitude then, I was obliged to follow suit. But this book is entirely a work of the imagination, and its Sunset Manor bears no resemblance whatsoever to any actual institution.

ONE

In moments of doubt and anxiety Miss Ormsby had always relied on Art to pull her through. During difficult times there was always comfort in recalling Schubert, which Miss Ormsby's small, frail mother had often played on the Heintzman on Sunday afternoons sixty-five years ago. *Gretchen at the Spinning Wheel.* Miss Ormsby's mother, who was of German descent, had explained how the story came from Goethe's *Faust.* Gretchen, a village maiden, is astonished to discover that the great Faust himself is smitten by her. The burden of his love weighs heavily on the girl, who sings "Mein Ruh ist hin, Mein Herz ist schwer." The voice of Miss Ormsby's mother always wavered in the dark parlour that smelled faintly sour from old lemon oil. She was not a strong vocalist.

At her spinning wheel Gretchen is overwhelmed by the great man's bearing and nobility. She describes her beloved. "Sein hoher Gang, Sein edle Gestalt." And then his kiss! "Und ach, sein Kuss!" Miss Ormsby's mother had always shivered with happiness over this passage. So had Miss Ormsby. In lighter moments they enjoyed the music of Albert W. Catellbi. *Sanctuary of the Heart. In a Monastery Garden. We'll Gather Lilacs in the Spring Again.* Miss Ormsby had stood by the Heintzman turning the pages of the

1

songbook for her mother. There was also, of course, the enchantment of poetry.

> *The splendour falls on castle walls*
> *And snowy summits old in story:*
> *The long light shakes across the lakes,*
> *And . . . .*

In the back seat of the taxi that was bearing her to Sunset Manor Miss Ormsby frowned. Her pale, narrow face looked grieved as she tried to summon up Lord Tennyson's absent line. Where had it gone? She could see it on page 95 of *Highways to Learning*. Miss Ormsby closed a watering eye. *And the wild cataract leaps in glory.* Of course! She knew the poem by heart and must have recited it a thousand times, standing by the tall windows that over-looked the football field. *The long light shakes across the lakes.* When the heart was full, the magic of such lines could take your breath away. And often did. What if most of them had returned only looks of blankness and boredom? There were always a precious few for whom such beauty was as vital to life as meat and drink. To remember and cherish such things was, Miss Ormsby believed, salutary.

The problem, however, was remembering things. In early June she had suffered a stroke, and now there were occasional lapses, darkening rooms in her memory where the lights only flickered and sometimes went out alto-gether. Dr. Carswell had told her not to worry about any of this; the memories of stroke victims, he assured her, were often fully restored. Yet it had to be borne in mind, he went on, that time took its toll on everyone. A certain amount of memory loss inevitably accompanied advanced years. Along with a host of other calamities, he added with a tired smile. In his heavy joking manner the young doctor pulled no punches with his elderly patients. Listening to all this Miss Ormsby had nodded her head of frizzy reddish hair and said nothing. What, after all, could one say? How could one disagree with the man? In his shopworn phrases dwelt the truth of our decline. *All flesh is grass.*

It was, however, distressing to someone like Miss Ormsby who had always valued the life of the mind over coarser pursuits. Only the other day, for instance, while filling in a crossword puzzle, she had been unable to command the first name of a famous seventeenth century essayist. She was certain that it was Philip, and yet Philip Bacon clearly didn't fit the puzzle and she had been forced to consult the encyclopedia. It was all very dismaying. Forgetting the name of a seventeenth century essayist was one thing; fire was quite another matter. Over the summer she had got into the habit of forgetting where she had put lighted cigarettes. These forgotten cigarettes would burn down until they fell from the lips of ashtrays to roll under chairs or lodge behind cushions. It was hazardous, and one Saturday morning in August, a fire in the kitchen had sent Miss Ormsby into the street appealing for help.

Within minutes the firemen arrived and pulled through the side door the smoking davenport upon which Miss Ormsby's dying father had lain during the last weeks of his life thirty years ago. The firemen doused the sofa with their extinguishers and left it in the driveway, a sodden and peculiar ruin that gave off a foul smell to the neighbours who had gathered to watch. Later that day George Scully came by with his truck and hauled the old couch away to the landfill site outside of town.

Standing that morning in the driveway by the lilac bushes, their flowers shrivelled and brown (Miss Ormsby no longer felt safe mounting the step ladder to snip them off when they had had their day), she endured a lecture from the young fireman who seemed to be in charge. He stood next to her in his rubber boots, canvas coat, and great peaked hat. There was an axe jammed under the belt of his coat, and with his large bushy moustache, he looked as fierce as a Tartar. No doubt he meant to be helpful, but nevertheless he was stern with her. "Careless smoking can get you into a lot of trouble Ma'am," he said. "If this had happened in the middle of the night, I wouldn't be talking to you like this. We'd be looking for what's left of you in the ashes." Frowning at her, he had stroked his big moustache, and Miss Ormsby had felt as foolish and as chastened as an errant child as she stood in the driveway in an old housedress that had seen better days. Her stockings were rolled down and bunched about her ankles. She went around the house like this in the summer, but it was no way to be seen by the neighbour-hood. The young fireman had been a terrible scold. "You should give them up," he said. "I did. Five years ago. You'll really feel better once you do."

Well, maybe I will and maybe I won't, Miss Ormsby had thought later while airing out the kitchen. The heat had blistered one wall, and the thought of finding someone to repaint the room was too fatiguing to consider. Instead she sat at the kitchen table with the door and windows open and lit another Benson and Hedges. She also had a large glass of Dry Sack. Well, who didn't need a pick-me-up after such an ordeal? In her lap lay her father's old pipe ash-tray—a miniature tire, glass-bottomed and inscribed with the words *Hallam Motors, Graham-Paige Sales and Service. Moreton, Ontario Phone 155.* Miss Ormsby had vowed to be more attentive and carry the little ashtray with her when-ever she felt like a cigarette in the house. But that was months ago and she had to concede that she often forgot. Perhaps it *was* time to go.

Now she looked out the taxi window at a late December afternoon the colour of old stones. It had been a peculiar fall with some snow in late October. Then the weather turned English and several mild damp weeks had left the town and countryside bare. At this time of the year everyone used to complain about the onset of winter.

4

Everyone in the staff room was glum about the months ahead. But really she had never minded the winter. You had to make do, was how Miss Ormsby always looked at it; each season provided its own unique delights. Why confine one's admiration to the charms of May or the lazy pleasures of July?

She used often to reflect on this while she shovelled herself out after a snowfall. At daybreak in February, with the morning star glittering in the pale sky, Miss Ormsby would be bundled up in boots, coat, scarf, and tam. Wearing a pair of leather mittens over woollen gloves, she would clear a path from her side door to the street. Men greeted her on their way to the shipyard or the flour mill. After shovelling herself out, Miss Ormsby had her oatmeal and coffee and cigarette before gathering up her books for school. In the evenings she ate her supper while reading a library novel. Then she graded papers at the kitchen table, sometimes reading aloud from an essay that seemed, in the glare of the yellow kitchen light, fresh or arresting. After several hours, the oilskin cloth of white and orange squares would score the pale soft flesh of her arms. The wind blew snow as fine as sugar against the windows and the big oaks and maples along Park Street creaked.

Before going to bed Miss Ormsby went down to the cellar, her dress tucked into rubber boots. There she heaped four or five shovelsful of coal into the big red clinkers in the mouth of the monstrous old furnace. And she waited for the lethal gases to burn away so she could bank things down for the night. There was immense satisfaction in performing these chores, and it was there in the basement that she enjoyed her last cigarette of the day. In those times, as she recalled, a Black Cat Cork Tip. Above and around her the north wind blew, and Miss Ormsby liked to imagine it as illustrated in children's books, a fierce-looking fat-cheeked ogre besieging her house. On such nights this coziness by the furnace was delicious.

When blood is nipp'd and ways be foul
Then nightly sings the staring owl
                    To Whit
To who!—a merry note
While greasy Joan doth keel the pot.

Her imitation of the owl always hastened laughter, and she supposed, to be fair, that she had looked rather odd with her eyes widened and her lips pursed for owl sounds. But you had to bring the written word to life. Poetry was meant to be dramatized, and the essence of good teaching was performance. She could remember Dr. Kettleheim saying that at the Teacher's College and that would have been in 1936. To whit! To who!

Miss Ormsby now noticed the young taxi driver's face in the rear view mirror. He was staring at her. "I beg your pardon," she smiled, "but I was remembering some poetry. By Shakespeare. In *Love's Labour's Lost.*" From behind, the young man's ponytail was fastened with rubber bands. He reminded Miss Ormsby of an Apache warrior. "I used to teach English," she said. "At the high school. I was there nearly forty years."

The young man nodded and Miss Ormsby, who had leaned forward to speak to him, settled back. They were now nearly there and she began to fish in her handbag for money. She could not abide women who waited until the last minute in grocery store check-out lines to find money for their purchases. It was inconsiderate to keep others waiting. Men, Miss Ormsby had noticed over the years, particularly resented such behaviour, and with good cause. As she searched through her bag, she withdrew the rubber ashtray advertising Graham-Paige motor cars. How on earth, she wondered, had that got into her purse? For the life of her, she couldn't remember putting it there but obviously she must have done. Dr. Carswell, though inclined to levity when dealing with her problems, would not

6

have been amused to learn that she carried an ashtray with her. He was after her to give up cigarettes. "You have high blood pressure Miss Ormsby," he kept reminding her. "I'm sure an intelligent woman like you realizes that smoking is bad for hypertension."

She knew that, of course, but how does one give up the habits of a lifetime? She had smoked cigarettes every day of her life since an evening in June 1934 when Gladys Springer offered her a Turret outside the Parkview Pavilion. That was over fifty years ago. So she took pills for her blood pressure and these kept her running to the toilet. That was a nuisance, but what after all could one do about such things except carry on.

They passed the shopping plaza along Transit Road and turned into the parking lot of the buff-coloured building. *Facility* was what Mrs. Rawlings had called it. "Welcome to our *facility*!" What a name for a place to call home! Miss Ormsby could remember when this part of town was all meadow and wild apple trees. It was called Parker's Fields. On Sunday mornings in early June she and her father would come out here to pick morels. Her mother gave them a huge enamel pot and they filled this with the edible fungi. Her tall solemn father always dressed like a bookkeeper. He would hang his suit coat upon the branch of a tree and search for the morels in his white shirt, vest, and trousers. His sleeves were kept in place by arm gaiters severely black and he wore a straw hat. As she squatted in the wet grass, Miss Ormsby used to marvel at the sunlight on spider webs. For minutes at a time she would gaze at the delicate filaments and at the insect toiling and spinning like some creature in a Biblical metaphor. It was a happy time and she wrote poems in her head and picked wildflowers for her mother, standing up now and then to ease her legs and watch her father, a white-shirted figure stooping in the grass. And now it was all under asphalt and automobiles, she thought as she stepped from the cab. The traffic along Transit Road hurtled past her.

Miss Ormsby paid the driver through the window, leaning forward to study the face beneath the ridiculous hair. Her eyesight was still good and there was something familiar about the young man's narrow sharp face. He had about him the look of a ferret and he was quite possibly a Wagner. She had taught several Wagners over the years; most of them had never made it past Grade Nine. Miss Ormsby thought she might have taught this young man's father. Or for that matter, his grandfather. Such people married young and bred early. "Are you a Wagner by any chance?" she asked. "That's right," the young man said, "how did you know?"

Miss Ormsby examined her change. Taxi fares nowadays were outrageous. How could anyone afford them? She handed the young man a quarter. "You look like a Wagner. Who was your father?"

"Jack Wagner," the young man replied.

"I don't remember a Jack. I taught a Joe Wagner once. He was a bit of a scamp." Leaning into the taxi had produced a crimp in Miss Ormsby's back and now she straightened up. "That would have been Uncle Joe," said the young man. "My old man never made it to high school."

Miss Ormsby nodded and stood for a moment, watching as the taxi drove off and entered the traffic along Transit Road. Across the highway the plaza was already crowded with afternoon shoppers. Miss Ormsby's trunk and phonograph and books had been sent ahead earlier in the week; now she had only her valise to handle. It was made of black pebbled leather and looked like a large doctor's bag. Miss Ormsby's father used to call it his grip. Hefting the bag in one hand, Miss Ormsby started across the parking lot to the entrance of Sunset Manor.

In the Sun Room Mrs. Lucas sat in one of the orange chairs looking out the window towards the parking lot and the gray afternoon. Mrs. Lucas had been thinking about Heaven, wondering in fact what a person would do there all day. Or all night for that matter. Or were there such divisions of time as day and night? Perhaps not. After all, why would you need to divide time into day and night? On the other hand, if there were no night, would it always be day? Or something altogether different? In one of his programs Pastor Bob had said that such matters were beyond the scope of human comprehension.

Such speculations he said belonged in a realm unvisited by mortals. God's palace was beyond the words of man, and it was fruitless to ponder the shape and dimension of His Heavenly abode. How the man could talk when he got going, thought Mrs. Lucas. Yet remembering his words she felt unfilled. The words of Pastor Bob were sometimes as thin and unsatisfying as the soups served up by the kitchen in Sunset Manor. She always longed for more. One bowl certainly didn't fill her up and there was no talk of seconds. When thinking of Heaven, Mrs. Lucas longed for concrete images; she yearned for pictures of the divine lifestyle. As a child she had been told by someone (her mother perhaps? She could no longer remember.) that the porches of the Lord's house were solid gold, His windows fashioned from rubies and emeralds, mother of pearl and amethysts. Mrs. Lucas loved the sound of these opulent words even though she had never laid eyes on such gems.

Staring out at the gray afternoon Mrs. Lucas wondered if you ate in Heaven. She already felt hungry and the biscuits and tea were still a half hour away. She hoped there would be food in Heaven, though to be perfectly fair, perhaps you didn't need it. Suppose you existed on air or something. Or drank a cup of golden elixir and that did you for a week or a month. Like those liquid diets she sometimes read about in the *Enquirer*. The thought of such fare, however, was mildly depressing.

It was very likely, she surmised, glancing at the piano in the far corner of the Sun Room, that there would be hymn singing, though perhaps not around a piano. There would doubtless be harps. Mrs. Lucas was troubled in her mind by the naked truth, and this was that she preferred piano music to the sound of a harp. They had a harp on the *Call of Tomorrow* program. A pale young woman in a gown sat on a stool, and with her long white fingers plucked the stringed instrument. It was nice enough, but when all was said and done, Mrs. Lucas was partial to the piano. Mrs. Lucas thought about the young woman in the long dress, her hands running up and down the strings of the harp like two small animals while the choir sang.

There were a number of black men in the choir and they had beautiful voices; there was no doubt about that. Black men could sing and run like the wind. That was common knowledge, and no doubt there were some good ones, though a considerable number seemed to be murderers and worse. Mrs. Lucas hoped there would be no black men in Heaven. Although she had never met one in the flesh, Mrs. Lucas was fairly certain that she would feel uncomfortable in his presence. And the thought of sharing eternity with one was insupportable.

Thinking about this eventuality she allowed that a few black women might be all right. Someone like the big fat woman in the long dress and bandana. The one who looked like Aunt Jemima on old syrup bottles. She was the woman who fussed over Scarlett O'Hara and got her ready for the ball where she met Clark Gable. Mrs. Lucas could remember seeing *Gone With the Wind* at the Capitol Theatre. It was during the war and it played for an entire week. People lined up along King Street clear to the Chinaman's laundry. She knew for a fact that some women saw the picture two or three times.

In her chair in the Sun Room Mrs. Lucas wondered if Clark Gable was in Heaven. She'd read somewhere in a movie magazine years ago that, like most Hollywood stars, Clark Gable had had his wild side. He chased women and probably drank. She couldn't remember now whether he'd gotten religion at the end. But even if he hadn't, didn't the Lord forgive sinners their transgressions? Pastor Bob often quoted the Bible to that effect. "There is more joy in Heaven over finding one sinner than in hearing about a host of the righteous." The words went something like that.

Mrs. Lucas stirred from her reverie about Clark Gable in Heaven and looked beyond the window. A taxi had pulled into the parking lot and discharged a passenger. She was a tall thin woman in a cloth coat. To Mrs. Lucas, the woman looked to be wearing some manner of frizzy orange hair. A wig, on the face of it. Or was it? It was hard to tell, but the effect was startling just the same. What kind of person would wear such a thing on her head? Earlier in the week Mrs. Lucas had watched a man carrying boxes and a large trunk through the front door. Perhaps those articles belonged to this woman with the orange hair. Mrs. Lucas was enlivened by the prospect of a new resident, and she looked around the Sun Room for someone to share the news with.

In a corner there were three people sitting in front of the television watching a serial drama. Mrs. Lucas recognized Mrs. Huddle and Mrs. Somers and Lorne Truscott. He watched the afternoon shows because he liked to look at the young actors and actresses kissing and hugging one another. Mrs. Lucas watched Lorne Truscott staring at this nonsense. His mouth was open and the loose flesh on his turkey neck was quivering. He looked, she thought, foolish beyond words. One night not long ago Mrs. Lucas had dreamed that Lorne Truscott fell down the main stairs and broke his turkey neck. He had died, but not before he had twitched for several moments like a dog she had seen run over by a dairy wagon seventy years ago. In her dream Truscott's eyes had bugged out of his head.

Mrs. Lucas looked across the Sun Room at Mrs. Huddle and Mrs. Somers. They also enjoyed those trashy programs. Most of the others did too, but they looked at them in their own rooms. And wasn't that a foolish extravagance! thought Mrs. Lucas. Why pay for your own television when there was a perfectly good machine in the Sun Room? Not that there was anything worth watching on it aside from the *Call of Tomorrow* program and the Sunday afternoon hymn sing, which was very nice.

Mrs. Lucas looked back out the window, but the tall thin woman with the orange wig had disappeared. There was only the familiar empty parking lot. Mrs. Lucas turned her attention back to the TV watchers. For a moment she thought of getting up and going over and telling them about the new person who wore an orange hair piece, but she thought better of it.

The only other person in the Sun Room was Mrs. Fenerty, who was now levering herself out of the chair into which she had sunk. Mrs. Fenerty was the oldest resident of Sunset Manor. She had now been on the planet for nearly a century, and she moved about in a cumbersome fashion with the aid of a chromium walker. But even with that device she usually needed assistance. The nursing staff was ever anxious for Mrs. Fenerty's safety, fearing that a fall might prove fatal. Her brittle old bones might break into pieces at the slightest mishap. Accordingly, the nurses were solicitous towards her; she had become something of a pet to them. They were proud that she had survived the worry and turmoil of nearly a hundred years and was now living out her last days under the roof of Sunset Manor. It was, they all agreed, a remarkable achievement.

Even now, as Mrs. Lucas watched, Nurse Haines appeared. She seemed to have a sixth sense about Mrs. Fenerty's wishes, and she would appear the moment the old woman moved. Now she helped Mrs. Fenerty lean into her walker and accompanied her as she made her slow, painful way out of the room. "All right now, Granny," said Nurse Haines, "steady as she goes." Mrs. Lucas watched them make their way out of the Sun Room and proceed along the corridor to the elevators. Observing them Mrs. Lucas could have cried aloud, for she so badly wanted to tell someone about the woman with the orange wig. But there was no one around to listen.

In his room on the third floor Mr. Wilkie was dreaming again of pretty girls and parallelograms. He had been watching the afternoon traffic but had fallen asleep in his chair. His window overlooked the shopping plaza across Transit Road, and although he had watched the traffic every afternoon for the past two years, he was still astonished by the number of women who now drove automobiles. As usual his eyes had grown heavy at this exercise and had finally closed. And once again he was in a white space filled with the quadrilateral figures that had always been his favourite geometric design. The parallelograms looked like the frames of new houses that had been blown askew in a gale. And in the middle of them the school girls wore angora sweaters and tartan skirts that were held in place by outsized safety pins. The girls wore their hair drawn back in ponytails that displayed their pretty necks. Their long slender legs were bare except for ankle socks and saddle shoes. They were unfastening their large safety pins when, to his dismay, Mr. Wilkie awakened, conscious only of a feeble stirring in his loins.

The puzzle book lay open on his lap. A year or so ago he had stolen the book from the public library, slipping it under his big winter coat and escaping undetected. Why he had suddenly decided to take the puzzle book was a mystery that he had grown tired of trying to solve. He no longer even thought about how the book had come into his possession; he merely acknowledged the fact that it now belonged to him and lay in his lap.

At some point in the afternoon he had been working on a problem in arithmetic involving the sale by one farmer to another of various commodities that were measured in bushels and pecks. Mr. Wilkie enjoyed working with this old-fashioned terminology; he liked to imagine that it kept his mind alert. Looking down from his window he saw the taxi enter the driveway of Sunset Manor and stop in the parking lot. From his window Mr. Wilkie could see only a portion of the parking lot at the side of the building, but he could see a frizzy-haired woman emerge from the taxi. She placed her luggage on the asphalt and settled her account with the driver.

As Mr. Wilkie arose from his chair for a better view, the puzzle book fell to the floor and Mr. Wilkie's half-moon reading glasses, attached to his ears by a black cord, were left to dangle across his chest. At the window he presented a tall, stooping figure in shapeless gray flannels, white shirt with bow tie, and blue cardigan sweater. He had always been a thin man, but during these last years, he had grown so spare that his clothes merely hung upon his frame. There appeared, for instance, to be no buttocks within his baggy trousers. In his left ear Mr. Wilkie wore a pearl-coloured button, and this instrument enabled him, when he so wished, to hear better. His eyesight for distance, however, was still good, and he now believed that he recognized the woman from the taxi.

As he looked down, Mr. Wilkie was certain that the woman was Kay Ormsby. But what on earth, he wondered, was she doing here? She couldn't be visiting someone, else why was she carrying a bag? Mr. Wilkie pressed his face against the glass, but Miss Ormsby had already disappeared beneath him; presumably she had entered the front door. The old man watched the taxi back up and then drive away, entering the traffic along Transit Road.

Settled once again in his chair Mr. Wilkie recalled the day that Kay Ormsby arrived at the high school. It was during the war and several men on the staff had joined the forces. That summer he had heard that there was to be a new female teacher in the English Department, and during the hot weeks of July and August, while mowing the grass, or serving iced tea to Ada in her chair, Mr. Wilkie imagined someone who might transport him. He dreamed of a woman who would read poetry to him or behave in an outrageous fashion; a theatrical type of person who would lose her heart to him and teach him the lessons of love. Ideally she would be French or maybe Hungarian, and wear black stockings and a beret. Perhaps she might have once been on the stage.

While he brought his wife her iced tea, Mr. Wilkie saw himself and the new English teacher in a variety of sexual embraces. For years Mr. Wilkie had been hoping that something passionate and extraordinary would happen to him, as it once did during his first year of teaching at a continuation school in the country. There an older woman who taught the first four grades had befriended and then seduced him in the cloakroom during recess.

It was a winter morning, and from the snowy playground the cries of the children were borne to the two figures maneuvering under a bundle of heavy coats and mufflers. Amid galoshes and rubber boots, Mr. Wilkie and the woman had thrust against each other in a fierce and quiet frenzy. The act was performed standing up with Mr. Wilkie gripping the steel coat hangers lest his trembling legs fail him. All this time he was fearful that a child, in search perhaps of a mislaid scarf or mitten, would come upon them. Such a discovery would almost certainly have meant the end of his employment and the unlikelihood of a suitable reference from the principal, whom Mr. Wilkie could hear making tea at the hot plate on the other side of the wall, Yes, the danger had been authentic, but also rather exquisite. Beneath his partner's dress was a kind of corseted encumbrance which required her help to unfasten. But she wore no underpants! An amazing revelation to Mr. Wilkie, who was only twenty-two at the time and who had been, at breakfast that morning, a virgin. Some weeks later the poor woman took ill; some said she had tuberculosis. In any case her husband kept her home and Mr. Wilkie never saw her again. At the end of the school year, he left for a better position, still somewhat anxious that he might have contracted the bacillus.

That encounter in the cloakroom scored his imagination forever, and so he was disappointed when he first laid eyes upon Kay Ormsby on that September morning when Mr. Pigeon called the staff to order with the reciting of the Lord's Prayer and a plea for the safety of the troops in Europe and the Far East. In those days Kay Ormsby was a plain, tall girl with red hair. She was pleasant enough, but she was not someone Mr. Wilkie imagined spending a rapturous Sunday afternoon with. It seemed to him that the young woman who had returned from the city to live with her father on Park Street was already an old maid, though she couldn't have been out of her twenties when she arrived.

He couldn't remember her having any boyfriends, though she spent a great deal of time one year with a young blond man who came on staff. He was an Englishman, and everyone wondered what he was doing in Canada and why he wasn't in the service. Mr. Wilkie could no longer recall his name, but it turned out he was queer. There was some kind of scandal involving a boy in the showers at the Y.M.C.A. Old Pigeon ran the Englishman out of town in a hurry. Later Kay Ormsby became friends with that poisonous woman Adelaide Bales. The two of them often took summer vacations together, and from time to time Mr. Wilkie was moved to wonder if there wasn't something untoward about that relationship. Two old maids in a feather bed and all that. He had never been certain, and now, in any case, it didn't matter. Adelaide Bales was dead. As were so many others.

Yet if Kay Ormsby were coming to live at Sunset Manor, she must be an age too. It was strange but he had always thought of her as someone much younger. But when he considered the matter, he supposed that there were fewer than ten years between them. It was frightening sometimes to think of how old he had become. In his chair Mr. Wilkie produced a tremendous yawn. He supposed his blood sugar was low and he wondered what was on for supper. For a moment he got up and stood by the window looking serious and watchful. Then he sat down again and returned to his puzzle book, where a merchant was trying to determine the cost of a recent shipment of goods that had arrived in hogsheads and firkins and other wooden casks of various sizes.

Lorne Truscott watched the young blonde kiss the doctor. She was a real looker and hot to trot. She was putting more into the kiss than the doctor, but then he was a bit of a sap in Lorne's opinion. This doctor wanted to marry the girl and make an honest woman of her, but all she wanted was some sack time. She'd already had plenty with Lorne's favourite character, a good-looking black-haired guy with a big moustache. And a big something else too probably. He was screwing nearly every woman in the show. He'd knocked up the blonde some months back and this doctor had performed an abortion on her.

Beside Lorne Mrs. Huddle had fallen asleep, her breath whistling faintly through her half-open mouth. Mrs. Somers, however, was still with it, if her blank stare meant anything. But she could have been dead the way she looked, thought Lorne. Now the blonde and the doctor stopped kissing. It hadn't been much of a kiss anyway. When the moustache used to kiss her, they'd be on the sofa and he'd ruffle her feathers. But all this sappy doctor seemed to want to do was talk. That was the problem with these goddamn shows. There was too much talking. Lorne watched the blonde leave the doctor's office. God Almighty, but she had a pair of legs on her! Then the commercials came on. That was another thing. They were always breaking up the story to advertise stuff, though he had to take a piss anyway. The old waterworks weren't what they used to be. It seemed that he was now up half the night staring at the toilet bowl and watching himself dribble into it. According to the quack there was a blockage in his system. Carswell had drawn him a picture on a prescription pad. There was some kind of gland in the middle of your arse about as big as a chestnut. Lorne couldn't remember what it was called. Carswell explained that as you got older, this thing got bigger and blocked off the flow from your bladder. Sometimes they had to operate on you, though as far as Lorne was concerned, it would be a frosty goddamn Friday in July before he let them put a knife into his backside.

He looked across the room at Mrs. Lucas, who was staring out the window. Maybe it was time to send her another giant pizza or a Chinese dinner for twelve. He had been warned, however, by Rawlings, so he guessed he'd better be careful. Placing his hands on the arms of his chair, Lorne heaved himself to his feet, and performed a peculiar little shuffle, snapping the police braces that contained his plaid shirt and held up his tan work pants. At this commotion Mrs. Huddle opened her eyes to appraise him briefly. Mrs. Somers, however, continued to stare at the television. "I have to go and bleed my lizard, ladies," said Lorne. The two old women nodded without looking at him.

18

TWO

"My dear Miss Ormsby," said Mrs. Rawlings. "It gives me enormous pleasure indeed to welcome you to Sunset Manor. How delighted we are to have you with us. Do come into my office and sit down. Your unit is ready and waiting, but first we must have a little chat and get acquainted. I shall be with you in a jiffy." Miss Ormsby had set down her valise by the secretary's desk and now allowed herself to be escorted into Mrs. Rawlings's office where the hearty woman patted her arm and left.

Clutching her handbag Miss Ormsby sat in a chair. From the other side of the door came the voices of Mrs. Rawlings and her secretary. The two women were conferring on a matter that appeared to involve an overdue account. Supermarket music played faintly in the background. Something to do with raindrops falling on people's heads. Miss Ormsby sighed. She supposed she would have to get used to such things, but already she missed the reassuring creaks in the timbers and floorboards of the old, dark house on Park Street. She was determined, however, to put a good face on this whole business. *A cheerful countenance aids the failing heart,* her mother used to say.

Mrs. Rawlings's office was comfortable enough with its

beige furniture and potted ferns. On the other side of the window, the traffic moved along Transit Road in the weak gray light of the December afternoon. Behind Mrs. Rawlings's desk were a small shelf of books and framed diplomas attesting to the fact that the administrator had passed courses in human relations and life management, whatever they were. Miss Ormsby arose to peruse the titles on the little shelf of books. *The Best Years Are Ahead. Living and Loving. The Dynamics of Aging. Successful Sex for Seniors.*

From time to time Miss Ormsby had glanced at such titles in the new books bin at the public library. Somehow though, these books, written by medical doctors and psychologists whose smiling faces appeared on the dust jackets, always left her mildly puzzled. Miss Ormsby's long bony face had always registered bewilderment as she encountered passages that were as obscure to her as the rites of heathen tribes. *If excessive corpulence presents a problem, it is often more comfortable for both partners if the female sits astride the male and inserts the member by hand.* To Miss Ormsby, a stranger all her life to ardent embraces, such instructions were as outlandish as messages in Urdu. She had always imagined that men and women performed the sexual act in a manner roughly similar to the stray dogs that used to attach themselves to one another on the streets of Moreton, the coupling animals looking dazed and intent, almost apologetic as they went about their business. One didn't see as much of that on the streets nowadays, and a good thing too.

Mrs. Rawlings now returned to her office, moving swiftly across the room to her desk. It was mildly frightening to see such a big person move with such haste and sense of purpose. Resting her plump arms on the desk she glanced at Miss Ormsby and then opened a buff-coloured file. "Well now," began the administrator. "I see that you smoke, Miss Ormsby." For a moment the light glanced off her glasses and hid her eyes.

20

"Yes, I do," said Miss Ormsby.

Mrs. Rawlings looked up from the file and smiled. It was, Miss Ormsby decided, an unpleasant smile, the gesture of a disapproving headmistress. "I'm sure you can appreciate," said Mrs. Rawlings, "that we do not allow smoking in the dining room or in the halls or in any of the recreational areas. When smoking in your unit, may I urge you to exercise extreme caution. Please bear in mind that nearly a hundred people live under our roof, and the hazards of fire are always uppermost in our minds."

"Of course," said Miss Ormsby.

Mrs. Rawlings again consulted the file folder. "Now what have we here? You have listed reading as your hobby. Reading and listening to music." Mrs. Rawlings looked up and again offered her bright false smile. "And over the years you have read to the blind. How very interesting, and I might add, laudable." Miss Ormsby's pale face flushed with embarrassment. "I don't know why I put that down. It was some time ago. I used to enjoy it. There were three or four elderly ladies in town with failing eyesight. They've since died, and nowadays the blind don't seem as interested in listening to someone like me read to them. They now have books on tape, you see. Read by professional actors. I have only one person who still prefers the company and she's nearly ninety. And last month she broke her hip and is now in the hospital."

Mrs. Hodgson! What a querulous old party she was! Nothing ever satisfied her. Her tongue was dipped in acid. Her poor husband must have suffered throughout their marriage. But the old woman loved good books. It was a relief to visit her and read from the works of the old masters. After Monica Dickens and Catherine Cookson, it was satisfying to read aloud from Henry James and Joseph Conrad. How odd that this starchy old woman, the widow of a bank manager in an Ontario town, should so enjoy listening to tales of the sea and of morally doomed men

21

who lived aboard ships. A genuine mystery there, thought Miss Ormsby. How fascinating and inscrutable most people were when you got to know them.

"Nothing else to occupy the spare moments?" asked Mrs. Rawlings. "I note that you have been an English teacher. Perhaps we can put your expertise to use in some group activity. Sunset Manor is not a nursing home, Miss Ormsby, but a facility for active, healthy seniors. We do have one or two residents who have a spot of trouble getting around, but in the main we encourage participation. We like to think that there is something for everyone at Sunset. We have theme dances, bridge evenings, costume parties, and exercise classes. The shuffleboard courts are in full operation during the summer months, and there is lawn bowling on the green, and the Sunset Choristers. Do you have a voice for song, Miss Ormsby?"

"I do not," said Miss Ormsby. "I love music, of course, but I fear I do not sing well enough for a choir."

Mrs. Rawlings made a thrumming sound in her throat that Miss Ormsby interpreted as denoting disapproval. "That seems a pity," said Mrs. Rawlings. "The Choristers are now at work on their Christmas program. They can always use another voice. However," Mrs. Rawlings added, "there are other activities. We shall almost certainly find something for you. We are not without amusements at Sunset. Everyone's birthday is celebrated with cake and candle. It is always festive in the dining hall during the evening meal. We encourage residents to socialize, Miss Ormsby. I myself have always believed that active participation promotes a good attitude and keeps the spirit fit. There is bridge, of course, and Mr. Wilson has, I believe, started a backgammon club. Some of the men prefer a good old-fashioned game of cribbage. There is bingo every Wednesday night and there are dances on Saturday if you want to trip the light fantastic. We offer both ballroom and square on alternate Saturdays, and Miss

Burchall teaches the rhumba and the tango. These have proven very popular with residents who remember such exotic steps from their youth."

Mrs. Rawlings wagged her large head as if constantly amused by such goings-on under her care. "Courtship can flourish, Miss Ormsby," she said. "You might be pleasantly surprised at how many of our residents find romance during their stay with us. We've had weddings under our roof, Miss Ormsby. On any night of the week, you may find Sunset couples at one of the cinemas in the Plaza or at The Chicken House, where, by the way, you are entitled, as a Sunset resident, to a special Senior discount on Tuesday nights. Just show the hostess your voucher. My secretary, Miss Crawley, has a generous supply of these."

Miss Ormsby listened as the administrator pointed out the nearby conveniences. There was an A & P, Drug World, Handy Cleaners, and Woolco. There were also three cinemas and a Pancake House. As Mrs. Rawlings listed the other stores in the plaza, Miss Ormsby looked out the window at the westering sun, a great yellow eye behind the clouds. She thought of time itself and the motion of immense spheres in space. At times like this it was comforting to ponder such large events. She also noted that Mrs. Rawlings's head was crowned with abundant hair that had once been auburn but was now tarnished with gray. A handsome woman nevertheless, and with a profile that might have once adorned a Roman coin. Emperor Rawlings! The woman probably meant well but she was too cheerful by half, prattling on about the meal hours and the laundry facilities.

The administrator's breezy manner put Miss Ormsby in mind of the young man from the real estate office who had hammered the For Sale sign into her lawn. The young man laughed a great deal (What was the joke? wondered Miss Ormsby.) and kept saying that her house would be easy to sell. People, he said, wanted older homes on quiet streets. And the trees! You couldn't get trees in the suburbs. And people were crazy about trees. When Miss Ormsby reminded him that the roof leaked and the plumbing was old, he just laughed. "No problem, Miss Ormsby, no problem." What did such an expression mean, she wondered. Dr. Carswell was another who was always saying "No problem," when surely *problems* were what he dealt with every day.

A cheerful countenance was one thing, but a foolish expression was quite another, in Miss Ormsby's opinion. These people reminded her of the young men who used to come to the door selling brooms and cleaning fluids when she was a child. They claimed to be working their way through college when they confronted her father at the door on a Saturday morning. He listened unsmiling as they offered up their company-directed greeting. "Good morning sir, I'm fine and dandy. How are you?" How awful it must have been in the evenings for those young men, alone in hotel rooms or tourist courts, writing up their orders and contemplating another day of "Good morning sir, I'm fine and dandy. How are you?"

Mrs. Rawlings was talking about churches. Sunday morning taxi service was available for Presbyterians, Anglicans, and Catholics. This service was gratis, provided through the kindness of the Rotarians. The Baptists had their own arrangements, and the Gospel Truth Centre had a bus that made regular stops. For the ailing, there were pastoral visits by various ministers and priests. If Miss Ormsby wished an appointment, Miss Crawley was the one to see. Miss Ormsby said, "I do not attend church, Mrs. Rawlings. Neither have I need for spiritual comfort from visiting clergy."

"To each his own, Miss Ormsby," said Mrs. Rawlings, closing the file. "Everyone is entitled to his own opinion, but may I just note in passing that during my twenty-five years of service in facilities like this, I have noticed that

some form of religious belief together with active participation lightens the load of our senior years. God and a
good bridge partner will see you through, as one resident
put it to me years ago. At the time she was ninety-three
years old, Miss Ormsby. And just as alert as you or I. She
attended church every Sunday and never missed a rubber
of bridge in all her years with us. You have to admit there
is something in it, Miss Ormsby."

"I admit no such thing, Mrs. Rawlings," said Miss
Ormsby. "It may have worked for the lady whom you refer
to, but such a regimen wouldn't do for me at all. From
roughly the age of fourteen, I have believed that God is
not to be found in churches or bridge clubs. He may be
found in a Beethoven sonata or a blade of grass or a poem
by Wordsworth. Or He may not. In any case I am still
looking for Him. I hope I may find Him before I die, but
I don't think it will be in a church."

Miss Ormsby felt a little breathless after this outburst.
She really hadn't intended to preach, but the big woman
had provoked her with this nonsense of bridge and God.
Mrs. Rawlings gave her a queer menacing look. "My dear
Miss Ormsby, let us hear no talk of dying. I cannot allow
such talk in the facility. It upsets the residents. It's quite
forbidden."

"But surely people here do die, Mrs. Rawlings," said
Miss Ormsby. "Given the average age, I would think you'd
see quite a lot of it over the course of a year."

Mrs. Rawlings raised a hand like a traffic policeman.
"Please! It is not a word we bandy about at Sunset." She
arose to stand in her great flat shoes. "And now, if you'll
excuse me, Miss Ormsby, I must get on with the business
of living. That's what we concentrate on at Sunset Manor.
Living! May I show you to your unit?" Miss Ormsby stood
up. We have taken a strong dislike to one another, she
thought, as she followed Mrs. Rawlings out of the office.

But all things considered, it probably could not have been avoided.

Mrs. Lucas gasped as the pain surged through her lower abdomen. For a moment it was intolerable and she leaned against the sink for breath. Deep within her a captive knot of air was seeking egress. This huge fist in her bowels was poised to strike. Moving forward slowly, Mrs. Lucas settled at last on the commode and broke enormous wind. Tears of relief filled her eyes. She should never have touched the cabbage at supper. Cabbage had never agreed with her and never would. Not in a thousand years could she expect to eat cabbage without discomfort. Yet in the dining hall she had been famished, and the portions were so meagre. Two bites took care of the cutlet, and an egg cup could have held the mashed potatoes. The boiled cabbage, however, had been plentiful, and she had partaken. Now payment was being exacted, for all was chaos within. Nor had it helped her digestion to reflect upon the fact that there was now in residence, and living next door to her, a woman who wore an orange wig. Perhaps, thought Mrs. Lucas, the woman had cancer and was being treated with chemicals. They said you lost your hair when you were treated with the chemicals. That would almost certainly account for the hair piece. Cancer! Mrs. Lucas shuddered and then produced another startling sound.

In the room on the other side of Mrs. Lucas, Lorne Truscott tapped along the wall like a fellow prisoner bearing messages. He sang from an old rock and roll song.

> *I hear you knockin'*
> *But you can't come in.*

During the construction of the facility, grasping contractors had skimped on materials, and so the walls in

Sunset Manor easily admitted nearby sounds; therefore, since Lorne Truscott's room was next to Mrs. Lucas's lavatory, he was privy to her most private acts. Sometimes he even inverted a glass tumbler against the wall, the better to hear her passing water or scrubbing her dentures.

Lorne Truscott was a nuisance to be sure, and Mrs. Lucas had many times requested a room change. Her pleas, however, had not moved Mrs. Rawlings to action. The administrator always cited the waiting list and the difficulty of transferring one's belongings at a certain age. As she remarked during one of these interviews, "People become attached to their units, Mrs. Lucas. They have their own little nicknames and personal treasures. You must bear in mind that Sunset is home now. The next step along the line is the Chronic Care Centre, and nobody I've met is in a hurry to go there. I will, however, have a word with Mr. Truscott. There really is no reason why you should be interfered with by a neighbor during your most intimate moments."

Mrs. Lucas doubted whether the administrator would have a word with Truscott. What did Rawlings know anyway? When it came right down to it, she was a great fat booby of a woman, and it was hard to understand how such a person was ever put in charge of the place. Before she left the bathroom, Mrs. Lucas loudly addressed the wall. "And how is your granddaughter these days, Truscott? Is there another little one on the way? And do you know who the father is?"

"When are you going to die, you old bitch?" cried Lorne Truscott.

"When I'm good and ready," Mrs. Lucas replied with evident satisfaction in her voice. Smiling at her riposte she went into her living room and sat down to read some pamphlets sent to her by the *Call of Tomorrow* people.

Mr. Wilkie sat in a booth in The Chicken House watching the waitresses in their blouses and short skirts and white shoes. They carried several plates of barbecued chicken at a time, balancing them on their arms. Others thrust soiled dishes and cutlery into bins that were wheeled away to the kitchen by weedy-looking youths. The clatter of it all was astonishing if you stopped to listen. Mr. Wilkie, however, had turned down his hearing aid. The waitress knew what he wanted. He came to the restaurant once a week, and ordered chicken salad, chocolate ice cream, and tea. He avoided Tuesday nights, when the place was filled with residents from the Manor.

The waitresses were mostly middle-aged women with stout legs. They were on the go all day, and when asked by Mr. Wilkie how they were faring, would usually complain of tired feet. That was understandable, and Mr. Wilkie would nod his head in sympathy. The waitresses fussed over him, and why not? He took a kindly interest in them, and though he was elderly, he was still presentable and mannerly. There were worse-looking men around than Arthur P. Wilkie. He glanced at his image in the dark glass of the restaurant window and saw a stoop-shouldered man in a blue blazer, white shirt, and gray slacks. He had tucked a maroon cravat around his neck.

There were people at the Manor who thought that he gave himself airs and was a bit of a dandy. But what of that? He had weathered the years better than most of them. Some of them frankly looked like hell as they shuffled around the place in their bedroom slippers and sweater coats. Mr. Wilkie had always dressed well. When she first met him, Ada had remarked on this. He was, she claimed, the nattiest dresser she had ever seen. And there was no denying that he had been the best-dressed teacher in the school. The pupils used often to mention it; the girls in fact flirted with him. "That's a nice shirt you're wearing this morning, sir." And so it had been!

He always wore Hathaway shirts and used cologne on his handkerchiefs. Personal hygiene was important too. He had scrubbed his teeth every day after lunch with Ipana. You couldn't be too careful about body odour and halitosis. It was astounding how many on the staff never considered such matters. In the late afternoon bad breath was rampant; it was worth your life to converse with some people. Others smelled. Mr. Wilkie remembered George Cuthbert, who taught biology. That man *stank*. One wondered if he ever took a bath. The pupils called him Stinky Cuthbert, and the poor beggar never caught on. It was amazing how obtuse some people were about these things. No, personal hygiene had always been foremost in Mr. Wilkie's mind.

Ada had also been fussy about odours. She always burned a match in the bathroom after number two. It was folly, however, to expect such consideration in the staff room. Adelaide Bales would come in from the gymnasium after leaping over the padded leather horse or maneuvering her Indian clubs. Still in her athletic togs and flushed and stinking of perspiration, she looked, Mr. Wilkie often thought, like a huge radish. Her friend Kay Ormsby had a peculiar odour about her too. She smelled of violets, perhaps, or lily of the valley. But the flowers were old and tired and reminded one of forgotten sachets in drawers or cedar chests. She was an old maid, of course, and carried about her the stale scents of spinsterhood. The perfumes and powders she used had once perhaps been Christmas presents.

Remembering these things, Mr. Wilkie thought of how Miss Ormsby was now a resident at Sunset Manor. Perhaps he should have gone around to her room and welcomed her to the place. It would have been the civil thing to do. Still, such a gesture was open to misinterpretation. You couldn't be too careful with the female of the species. It didn't take much to put ideas into their heads. He knew for a fact that he was not without his admirers; several ladies at the Manor had expressed an interest. But Mr. Wilkie was wary of entanglements. It wasn't long before they got their hands on your money and then where were you?

Miss Ormsby could not sleep. She had been lying in bed since ten o'clock and it was now half past one, and she had got up to stand by the window in her flannel nightdress. Her window overlooked the parking lot, and she stood staring down at the empty dark space. Now and then a car passed along Transit Road. The shopping plaza was deserted, though she could see the reflection of lights on the asphalt of the parking lot. It was still astounding to think that as a child she had wandered over these fields with her father on Sunday mornings. Now it was all beneath pavement.

Standing by the window reminded her of motels and of summer holidays with Addie Bales. They had gone to Nova Scotia or Virginia or some other place in Miss Ormsby's stout little bustle-backed 1952 Plymouth. Sometimes Miss Ormsby had a restless night, and so while Addie snored, Miss Ormsby had stood by windows watching the three A.M. truck traffic. In a few hours they would be on their way to a new town. *Tomorrow to fresh woods and pastures new.* The sense of impermanence and adventure had all been a bit thrilling on those summer nights thirty years ago. But this room overlooking this highway was different. This was now home.

She listened to the ticking of the Westclox on the dresser. Two years ago at Christmas her cousin Doreen had given her a digital radio clock, but Miss Ormsby had never got used to the thing. Lying in bed she had stared into the darkness at the little red digits as they silently and precisely marked off the minutes of her life; this experience had been, in some mysterious fashion, unsettling, and so the digital radio clock had gone into the cedar chest and, with other household goods, was eventually sold at auction.

Miss Ormsby now returned to her bed, though sleep continued to elude her. This was to be expected, of course, in new surroundings. She was now in her *unit*, as Mrs. Rawlings called it. And, when all was said and done, it wasn't such a bad place. It was small, however, and she already missed the roominess of the house on Park Street with its dark creaking wood and high ceilings. There had been cobwebs in the corners of those ceilings and dust on the furniture; she had never been much of a housekeeper, and she made no apologies for that. She could share space with spiders too.

The new owners had talked of changing things. Miss Ormsby had heard them as they walked about the house with the real estate man. The woman kept saying, "We can make that into a playroom for the children. We just have to knock that wall out." Miss Ormsby has listened with astonishment. *Knock a wall out!* It seemed such an outrageous thing to do. Miss Ormsby could see the falling plaster and old dust settling in the air. The noise and confusion of all that dismantling. And the walls were perfectly sound and useful in their present state. Of course it was not for her to say now. Papers had been signed, and the money for the house was in the bank. For a moment Miss Ormsby felt stricken with panic. She could no longer remember the names of the people who had bought her house.

She lay in bed confounded by this loss. Their names! Good Lord, if anyone asked who had bought her home, she would have no answer. She remembered that they had the same name as a band leader of long ago. That was how she often tied things together these days. It was called association. She had read about it in a book on strokes and sometimes it worked. Then it came to her. Dorsey! Their name was Dorsey. It was a small triumph over bewilderment, and in her bed, Miss Ormsby wiggled the toes of her long white feet and smiled. "I'm not ga-ga yet," she said aloud.

But where was blessed sleep? "Sleep that knits the ravelled sleeve of care," as great William put it. And who could have put it better? The dark winter daybreak was still hours away, but she would have to be up and about by nine. Evidently cleaning people came in to vacuum and dust and it wouldn't do to be seen in one's nightdress. One paid for this service, and as far as Miss Ormsby was concerned, it was welcome. There were better things to do in life than vacuum and dust. In the next room someone coughed. The walls in the place were like paper.

Earlier in the evening Miss Ormsby had put Brahm's A Minor on her phonograph. The music had soared, filling her with sadness and joy, the richness of existence itself. Without question, manna for the soul. "In the midst of desolation, my heart is uplifted by song." And Miss Ormsby had imagined her heart borne aloft by the music. Brahms! A very great man indeed. One of the immortals. With his beard and heavy face and thoughtful solemn eyes, he had stood beside Beethoven and Wagner in the steel engraving that hung above the Heintzman in the parlour. Mad Tchaikovsky was there too and Mozart and Mendelssohn and Father Bach and others. All were dressed in frock coats and looked like Victorian gentlemen at a board meeting. The picture had been her mother's graduation gift from the conservatory. Designed, Miss Ormsby imagined, to inspire the graduates.

The music of Brahms had stirred Miss Ormsby greatly until there had come a knocking on the door, and she was confronted by her neighbor peering in at her. Sniffing the cigarette smoke and asking if Miss Ormsby would mind turning down the music. She was a short stout woman with a froggy look about her. The large head and protruding eyes put one in mind of amphibious life. The hands were speckled with age. There were dozens of women like her in town. Miss Ormsby had taught their children and their grandchildren, and always she could detect a sign of kinship: the cast of an eye or the shape of a mouth. Even though the years had done their frightful ravaging work, there was yet something to recognize in a jaw or a brow. The woman had stared at Miss Ormsby's head in the most blatant way. It was the dull stupefied gaze of the ignorant; the gawking eye that cannot tear itself away from the growth on a neck or the stump of a severed limb.

After the woman left, Miss Ormsby had turned down the Brahms and smoked another cigarette. Music was a consolation and without it life was surely diminished. In the house on Park Street she had conducted Beethoven symphonies and Mozart sonatas, using for a baton a lacquered chopstick, a memento from a San Francisco holiday. These performances had left her spent and perspiring, but they had been, nevertheless, a feast for the heart. She supposed she would have to be careful lest people discover her and conclude that she was crazy.

For the second time Miss Ormsby got up and stood by the window. She felt as anxious as a child before a recital. In the morning she would have to eat with a hundred other people. For supper tonight she had made do with biscuits and cheese from her handbag, though perhaps they had a regulation about eating in one's apartment. But now, for the rest of her days, she would eat with other people. Like a child at boarding school. Only the child eventually graduates. Here one graduated to the grave, despite what Mrs. Rawlings thought of the matter. The notion of eating with other people was altogether novel to Miss Ormsby. It was not the meals themselves that caused concern; food had never been that important to her. She had always eaten what was available, scarcely aware of what it was since she was usually reading. Now she wondered whether reading while you are in the dining hall would be interpreted as rude. Very likely.

The night before, her last in the house on Park Street, she had expected to be awake most of the night. In fact, thanks to three large Scotches, she had slept soundly. That, however, had been a mixed blessing, for she had awakened with a hangover that hadn't disappeared until noon. Now she longed for sleep. By the window Miss Ormsby sighed. Desperate times called for desperate measures. Rummaging in her valise she withdrew a half-filled bottle of Johnny Walker and poured herself a generous measure, sprinkling a little tap water into the glass. Pulling a chair to the window, she sat down, and placing the rubber ashtray on the floor next to her, she lit up.

She would have to be careful; there must be no fires. She had put herself on an allowance of ten cigarettes a day, and this one would have to count against this new morning. The Scotch began to warm her and she felt at peace. A little alcohol was beneficial. It was supposed to open your arteries or something. Carswell had no objection to her having a drink now and then and had said as much. By the window she smoked and drank and began to feel happier. Life arranged itself around certain possibilities. We live on hope and the promise of tomorrow, thought Miss Ormsby, looking around her living quarters. She would make the best of it, and perhaps the best was not so bad. Once she and Addie Bales had been put into a perfectly dreadful room in a Mexican hotel. There were cockroaches and a bad smell from the drains. Adelaide was beside herself, but Miss Ormsby had told her that they could make the best of it. And why not? One could get used to nearly anything. It was all in the mind and the mind could not be invaded, thought Miss Ormsby, helping herself to another drink.

They had delivered her books. These were in cardboard boxes, and tomorrow she would arrange them somehow. Perhaps she would ask about some kind of shelving. And flowers! She would treat herself to some cut flowers. Music and books and flowers, the faithful companions of her life. And why should they abandon her now that she was living among a hundred others? She could still enjoy Brahms and Mozart, but at a reasonable level. Perhaps the stout woman with the froggy look had a point. You couldn't expect everyone to share your tastes. The truth was that precious few in town ever had. But what of that?

Miss Ormsby went to the tiny bathroom to water her third and final Scotch. She felt relaxed now. Sleep was not far off; another cigarette and then to bed. On her long narrow feet she walked across the room, and screwing shut one eye against the smoke, bent down and searched through one of the cardboard boxes. *Highways to Learning*. Of all the many texts she had used over forty years in the classroom, *Highways* was unquestionably her favourite. Published in 1939 and still a reliable guide to the treasures of the language.

> *She walks in beauty, like the night*
> *Of cloudless climes and starry skies;*
> *And all that's best of dark and bright*
> *Meet in her aspect and her eyes.*

Naughty Byron! But his words enchanted. Pacing by the window, Miss Ormsby smoked and read aloud.

> *And on that cheek and o'er that brow*
> *So soft, so calm, yet eloquent,*
> *The smiles that win, the tint that glows,*
> *But tell of days in goodness spent,*
> *A mind at peace with all below*
> *A heart whose love is innocent.*

On the other side of the wall someone flushed a toilet. Miss Ormsby put out her cigarette, finished her drink, and got into bed. Sleep was now not far away. The gentle darkness beckoned to her. She lay with her pale hands folded across her chest, wondering like a monk of old if this was how she would look in her coffin. Would she die in her sleep like her mother? Her tiny saintly mother who had died as quietly as she had lived. It was a March night in 1937. Miss Ormsby could still remember that. She was in her last few months of Teacher's College in Toronto. She had been reading when she was called to the telephone in the hallway of the rooming house. A long distance call was unusual. She could remember the old wall telephone with its cone-shaped receiver. Her father's voice was stricken with grief. "Kay! You'll have to come along home tomorrow. There's a train at seven in the morning. It's your mother. She's passed away. Just this evening. Not an hour ago."

Her mother! She hadn't been sick a day in her life except for the headaches that had plagued her from time to time. "She just came in from visiting the Nelsons," said her father. "I was listening to the radio. She said she had one of her headaches and was going to bed. So she went upstairs. And when I went in, she was gone." Her mother had only been in her early fifties. Miss Ormsby wondered if one day she too would be carried away like that; the victim of a faulty valve or a weakness in the lining of some arterial wall. At some moment a frayed artery bursts and sprays the brain with blood, plunging you into everlasting darkness. Something in her head had already gone astray and clouded her memory. She often felt a heaviness there; it was as though clouds were trying to disperse.

On this December night she lay waiting for sleep, thinking of death. Her father's too. That had been another fearful night. If you could survive such a night, then you could sleep alone in an empty house, unafraid, for the next thirty years. How he had cried aloud from the sofa in the kitchen that night! He had called for his dead wife. Upon awakening, Miss Ormsby had sat up in bed and listened to her father's voice travelling up the stairs from the kitchen. He had gathered his last strength to cry out in the night to his long dead wife. "Oh Mary! Oh Mary, I'm afraid."

Miss Ormsby had gone down at once, and after calling the doctor, had held her father's large, bony hands, the knuckles huge and white. His hands smelled of the sickbed and of the disease that was ravaging him. In his delirium and pain he called for her to turn off the kitchen light, and she had. And the last she saw of him was his glittering terrified eye. To hold the hand of your dying father in the darkness took strength. But she had been a strong young woman then. Miss Ormsby listened to a truck gearing down for the traffic light on Transit Road. This little motel room was now her home and she would get used to it. One could get used to anything. Purpose and conviction could banish gloom. Lord Tennyson had put it well.

Old age hath yet his honour and his toil
Death closes all: but something ere the end
Some work of noble note, may yet be done
Not unbecoming men that strove with Gods.

In the next apartment someone coughed. Miss Ormsby slept.

THREE

Mrs. Lucas watched Nurse Fox help Mrs. Fenerty into her seat at one of the tables. There was Christmas music on the loudspeakers this morning, and one day soon they were going to put up a tree in one corner of the dining hall. There was going to be a trimming party and that would be nice, though probably Lorne Truscott would spoil things with his off-colour stories and boisterous ways. Mrs. Lucas suspected that he kept liquor in his room.

Staring across the dining hall Mrs. Lucas decided that Mrs. Fenerty no longer looked quite human. This morning the nurses had braided her hair and put a horrible purple dress on her. They fussed over Mrs. Fenerty so much that they had no time for other residents. She was treated like someone special, and all because she was nearly a hundred years old. She should be in a nursing home, thought Mrs. Lucas. She was scarcely presentable in public. In her pigtails and purple dress she looked like some large ancient child. Mrs. Lucas watched the old woman spooning porridge into her mouth. Nurse Fox was patting her back. "Are you all right now, Granny?" asked the nurse. Mrs. Fenerty nodded her heavy old head.

It was only seven-thirty, but the dining hall was already filling up, for most of the residents of Sunset Manor rose early. Shifting her buttocks Mrs. Lucas considered the hour and her own tiredness. She had had a poor night of it. But what could you expect when your new neighbour turned out to be some kind of lunatic who moved about in the middle of the night talking to herself? With her own ears Mrs. Lucas had heard the woman chanting some strange gibberish. Maybe she belonged to one of those cults you read about in the *Enquirer*? How else could you account for someone going on like that in the middle of the night? Mrs. Lucas decided that she would have a word with Mrs. Rawlings about the matter. After all, she wasn't paying good money to be kept awake by some crazy woman who wore a wig and belonged to some cult. Mrs. Lucas decided that she would make an appointment with Mrs. Rawlings's secretary as soon as the office opened.

Lorne Truscott watched Mrs. Huddle shake some All-Bran into her bowl and pour milk over it. She must be having trouble with her crapper, decided Lorne. Thank God that part of him still worked. Mrs. Huddle put some of the mixture into her mouth and passed the box of cereal to Mrs. Somers. Lorne could see Mrs. Lucas behind his two dining partners. She was seated by herself and was looking around the dining hall. Looking for trouble more than likely, thought Lorne. Well, the old bitch was going to get some and very soon.

Everything had gone well; the people had been nice when he called. They promised to send a man over at the beginning of the week. It would be better than the time they delivered the chair to her. He had laughed for a week over that goddamn chair advertised on the television. Lazeeboy Lounger they called it. It took two men half an hour to get the son of a bitch into the elevator. Not a bad-looking chair either. But it was too big for her doorway even if she'd wanted it. He'd stood in the hall listening. How that woman raved, claiming she'd not ordered any chair and didn't even watch the televison program. He caught hell for that. Rawlings had the both of them into her office. She was just like some goddamn school principal with two kids. But he'd played his cards pretty close to his chest. Anyway, it wasn't his fault if she was so careless about leaving her credit card in the Sun Room. Showing off like that. Telling everyone how her son gave her a credit card for Christmas. Later he chopped it up with scissors and flushed it down the toilet. Rawlings had been in his room looking for it; he knew that for a fact.

Everyone listened as "Deck the Halls" was interrupted by Mrs. Rawlings's voice. "Good Saturday morning to all Sunsetters! This is Cora Rawlings speaking. It's a mild cloudy day with a temperature of thirty degrees Fahrenheit or zero centigrade. The weatherperson is forecasting snow for later in the day. And now the announcements. The Sunset Choristers will be singing carols in the dining hall on Tuesdays, Thursdays, and Saturdays during the noon meal. The Chamber of Commerce has also invited them to perform twice next week at the shopping plaza. Congratulations to Mrs. Henning and all the guys and gals.

"Today's program features a dancerize class in the gymnasium at ten. Miss Bonnie Cornet of the Moreton Y.M.C.A. is in charge and has asked me to remind class members to be on time. There is room, by the way, for new members. Wear leotards or exercise pants. A reminder however: you must have a note from your doctor before you can participate. The Great Books Club is meeting at two in the Seminar Room. Mrs. Featherstone asks you to bring your copy of *Hawaii*. You will be discussing Chapter Three. New members are always welcome. The dance committee has a meeting in Mrs. Rutlege's room at ten this morning. She would like to remind everyone that this week's theme is 'Down Mexico Way,' so put on your shirts and skirts for an evening of fun Mexican style tonight, beginning at eight. By the way, the dance committee needs volunteers to help decorate the gymnasium.

"Today's lunch will feature a tasty assortment of cold cuts and salad. Tonight we are offering a choice of home-baked beans and meat loaf or macaroni and cheese casserole. And now our thought for the day: *Today is the tomorrow you were worrying about yesterday.* Will the following people please pick up their medication in the infirmary by nine o'clock: Mrs. Bull, Mr. Wollinski, Mr. Doucette, Mrs. Huddle, and Mrs. Colborne. Have a nice day everyone!"

Mrs. Huddle leaned across the table towards Lorne Truscott. "What did she say about tomorrow and yesterday? I didn't catch that."

"Not to worry, Mrs. H.," said Lorne. "You've got to pick your dope up at the clinic by nine bells."

"Is that so?" said Mrs. Huddle, stirring the cereal in her bowl. "What dope would that be I wonder."

Lorne ate a piece of toast. His appetite wasn't what it used to be, but then what the hell was? And the food in the place didn't exactly make you want to bang your spoon on the table for more. Christ Almighty, he used to eat a plate of fried potatoes and eggs every morning, winter or summer. Now they only gave you eggs twice a week. They were supposed to be bad for your cholesterol or something. Everything was bad for you according to them. You shouldn't eat this, you shouldn't eat that. Lorne closed his fist on the piece of dry toast.

"What day are we again, Mr. Truscott?" asked Mrs. Huddle, leaning forward.

"Saturday, Mrs. H.," said Lorne. "We used to work Saturday mornings at the Foundry. And then we got paid. Sometimes we went on a toot toot toot. At the Royal Hotel. Do you remember the Royal? She's gone now. Torn down."

41

"Is that so?" said Mrs. Huddle.

"That is so, Mrs. H.," said Lorne, looking around the dining hall. She was leaving. Going up to do her after-breakfast business. Well, he'd wait that one out. He'd slip into the Sun Room and watch some cartoons. Tom and Jerry. Bugs Bunny. The Roadrunner. Beep Beep! He used to watch them with the kids on Saturday mornings. Tomorrow he would see the kids and Rhonda. It was something to look forward to. Along with the arrival of Lucas's new visitor. They said he'd be around on Monday or Tuesday. Smiling at Mrs. Huddle and Mrs. Somers, Lorne opened his hand and deposited the little pile of crumbs on the table cloth.

"Settling in then, are you?" asked Arthur Wilkie, as he spread marmalade on his toast with care. The confection was sticky and a nuisance if it got on your fingers. Mr. Wilkie could not help observing that Miss Ormsby had also selected toast, marmalade, and tea, and this information he found mildly upsetting.

"Yes, thank you, Arthur, I am," said Miss Ormsby, placing the library novel on the chair beside her. She had intended to eat breakfast alone with her book, but as chance would have it, she had entered the dining hall at exactly the same time as her former colleague. Both had gone to the serving area together to pick up their trays. They had then sat down at the nearest table; to do otherwise would have seemed unfriendly, perhaps even rude.

As she sipped her tea, Miss Ormsby watched Mr. Wilkie, who was using his knife and fork to cut his toast into tiny rectangles. Saturdays were for rectangles, while other days had their own geometric denominations. Meeting Arthur Wilkie like this was something of a shock for Miss Ormsby, because in fact she had thought he was dead.

42

It was nearly twenty years since his retirement, and she had scarcely heard of him in the interval. She imagined that it was at least a decade since she had seen him on the main street. His wife had been in her grave now for years; she had passed on while he was still at the high school. The poor woman had been an invalid. "Have you been here long, Arthur?" asked Miss Ormsby.

"No, no," Mr. Wilkie replied, forking a rectangle of toast into his mouth. He chewed the bread patiently, and with a paper napkin wiped his lips. "I just came in this minute like you. I just stepped off the elevator."

"I meant," said Miss Ormsby smiling, "at the Manor. As a resident."

"Oh!" said Mr. Wilkie. "I see." He thought about the question. "Not long. Three years next March. Or perhaps it was April. It was early spring in any case."

He brought the cup of tea to his lips, and Miss Ormsby noticed the mild tremor in his hands. Mr. Wilkie held the cup with both hands to avoid spillage. He had always been a handsome, vain man, and many a young girl had willingly become ensnared in the thickets of algebra and trigonometry, suffering defeat and failure, and all for the sight of Arthur Wilkie at the blackboard of a Monday morning. In those days he bore a startling resemblance to the band leader Harry James, who was married to Betty Grable, the starlet. And the sentimental young creatures felt sorry for Mr. Wilkie, whose wife was in a wheelchair. Miss Ormsby sometimes saw Ada Wilkie at community concerts. She was a thin birdlike woman with a faded prettiness. Arthur took her for drives in the country in his gray Dodge car on Sunday afternoons. One sometimes saw them passing by on their way out of town.

Arthur Wilkie was still handsome in his salt and pepper suit with a gray striped shirt and bow tie. Arthur had always been a careful dresser and he still was; certainly he was better turned out than the the other old men in the dining hall. Miss Ormsby watched Arthur Wilkie chew his toast; there was something fragile and delicate and rather beautiful about him. As he chewed and swallowed, the long blue vein in his temple throbbed behind the papery flesh. The fine white hair was still abundant. And he still had his little moustache. Yet he was so frail and old, and in his gray handsomeness, he looked like a . . .

The word that would complete the simile eluded her. It lay maddeningly close to the surface of her consciousness but could not be unearthed. It was frustrating to lose nouns like this. Dr. Carswell, of course, told her not to worry about it. In the demotic tongue of the age, it was "no problem." Just a mild form of aphasia, and perfectly normal after certain kinds of cerebral hemorrhage. The words, he assured her, would return. But it was frightening to Miss Ormsby, for without language she felt forsaken. She sipped her tea to calm the stirring in her heart.

She had always thought of Arthur Wilkie as much older, though when she considered it, he couldn't be more than ten years beyond her. When she arrived at the school, he would have been in his middle thirties. And that would mean he was now well into his eighties. She remembered him as a spare and rather haughty man. He wasn't well-liked in the staff room. Far too distant. Some thought him arrogant. Addie Bales, for one, could not abide him. "I can't bear that Arthur Wilkie," she used to say. If only Addie could see her now, thought Miss Ormsby. Having breakfast with, of all people, Arthur Wilkie! Life could certainly be strange and mysteriously unpredictable, she thought, smiling.

"You seem to have found something to be amused about," said Mr. Wilkie. Miss Ormsby looked down at her long pale hands. "Oh Arthur," she said. "I was just thinking how very odd it is that we should end up in a place like this."

Mr. Wilkie pondered this observation. "Odd? I don't see anything particularly odd about it. Why shouldn't we be here?" He laughed abruptly and rather nastily. "Where else could we go, for goodness sakes? I got tired of looking after my apartment, and presumably you found your house too much to handle. Neither of us has offspring. Where else could we go?"

"Well yes, of course that's all true," said Miss Ormsby. "What I meant though is that it's odd in the sense that if either of us had thought, say, thirty years ago . . ." Miss Ormsby always became excited over speculations of this nature: the ironies, the inexplicable paradoxes; these fundamental mysteries to be marvelled over and cele-brated. One encountered the strangeness of life with every passing day. "Suppose," she continued, smiling at Arthur Wilkie's pale stern face, "that I had said to you thirty years ago this very day, in the staff room, just as you were having your coffee and about to mark a set of tests. Suppose I had said to you, 'One day, Arthur, we will be having breakfast together in a retirement home west of the town limits where Parker's Fields now are.' Wouldn't you have thought that altogether strange?"

Mr. Wilkie gave her a queer look of dislike. "I should certainly have thought it strange. And why would you utter such a remark in the first place? I'm afraid I haven't the faintest notion what you're getting at."

"It's nothing, Arthur," said Miss Ormsby. "Mere idle speculation." She watched as he again brought his cup of tea to his lips. He seemed annoyed with her. He had turned into a waspish old man. A vague memory stirred within her. It had to do with a car full of soldiers in the school parking lot. The soldiers were drinking and some-one said they were waiting for Arthur Wilkie. It must have been during the war, and it had something to do with one of the soldier's wives. In those days Arthur Wilkie had the reputation of being a lady's man. Miss Ormsby had always thought it was only town gossip, but then on a winter afternoon there appeared that carload of soldiers. Mr. Wilkie spent an hour behind the closed door of Mr. Pigeon's office. Then the police arrived and sent away the soldiers. Allan was at the school that year, and he and Miss Ormsby had watched everything from her classroom window. Allan had been amusingly naughty about the incident. Poor Allan! She hadn't thought of him in a very long time.

Miss Ormsby ate a piece of dry toast. She was used to eating breakfast alone with a book, and now she was seated at a table at Sunset Manor with Arthur Wilkie. It was quite extraordinary how life could turn out. Neither of them, however, was enjoying the meal, and she would try to avoid him another day. She would get up a half hour earlier and be finished by the time he arrived. All in all that would be a more satisfactory arrangement.

Miss Ormsby's neighbour, the stout froggy-faced woman, was leaving the dining hall. She looked over at Miss Ormsby and nodded, unsmiling. I annoyed her with Brahms last night, thought Miss Ormsby, who could no longer remember the woman's name. I have not been in the place twenty-four hours and I have already irritated two people. Three, if one counts Mrs. Rawlings. After the stout woman passed, Miss Ormsby leaned forward. "Excuse me, Arthur," she said. "But do you know the woman who just passed by our table? She lives next to me on the second floor. I've forgotten her name."

Mr. Wilkie was arranging the dishes on his tray. "This place," he said, "is filled with women who are after your money. They'll do anything. I don't know that particular woman. I happen to live on the third floor. But I expect she is like the others. They flirt. They invite you to dances or to the chicken restaurant. Some of them ask you to go with them on coach trips to Florida. I keep my distance, believe you me."

With his salt and pepper suit and gaunt unhappy face Arthur Wilkie looked, Miss Ormsby thought, like a modern version of Hamlet's ghost. He looked like a *wraith*. That was the word she had wanted. *Wraith*. Its appearance was a small triumph, and she felt elated. However, in future, she would try to avoid Arthur Wilkie at meal times.

Mr. Wilkie lifted his brogues, allowing the housekeeper to pass the vacuum cleaner around his feet and under the chair. He had turned down his hearing aid against the noise of the machine. The housekeeper, a dark young woman of foreign extraction, nodded and moved away. Mr. Wilkie planted his heavy pebbled shoes once more upon the carpet. The housekeeper moved about his room while Mr. Wilkie watched her. He guessed that she was Greek or Italian. She moved briskly about while he sat in the chair with his puzzle book. Earlier he had watched her bend across the bed to change his sheets. She had quite the backside on her.

He never spoke to the woman or to any of the others. They dusted and cleaned his room, but he turned off his hearing device. Some of them sang while they worked; he knew this because he could see their lips moving. It didn't do, however, to get too friendly with them. Some of them had already buried husbands and were on the prowl. He'd heard of cases where elderly men had given themselves over to maids and housekeepers. It was an old story. And then, the next thing they were dead, and these women were living off the insurance. Taking their children to spend the summers in outlandish places like Bulgaria or Sicily. No, thank you very much, thought Mr. Wilkie. You couldn't be too careful. He watched the woman gather up her bulky apparatus and leave.

After she left, he turned on his hearing aid. In a minute there came to him the faint roar of the vacuum cleaner in the next room. Sitting in his chair by the window, Mr. Wilkie decided that he would have to change his dining habits. Old maids could be persistent; they could be difficult to thwart. It might take a determined effort to remain civil in her presence. Those smiles and that wild talk about the staff room thirty years ago. To the best of his knowledge he had never had any conversation with Kay Ormsby thirty years ago about living in a retirement home west of the town limits. Where would she get such an idea unless she had become deranged from years of sexual frustration?

There was a mild roaring in Mr. Wilkie's ears, and he adjusted the pearl-buttoned hearing aid before getting up to stand by his window. You dressed for the day and trimmed your moustache. You clipped the hair in your nostrils and applied shaving lotion. Unlike the other men, who shuffled about the place in bedroom slippers and old pants, you made an effort to be presentable in public. And they bothered you. Women outlived men by six or seven years at least, and there they were, ever eager to assail you.

On the outside of Mr. Wilkie's window the thermometer registered just below freezing. And they were predicting snow on the radio. There could be ice too. People would take tumbles; hips would crack and old bones would splinter. Last January at this very window he had watched a woman fall as she was getting into a taxi. She had slipped and broken something large, perhaps a leg. He had watched as they put a blanket over her, until the ambulance arrived with its red roof light turning. There was quite the commotion outdoors that morning. You never knew what could happen when the temperature dipped below freezing. You were safer indoors with numbers, thought Mr. Wilkie, drawing his chair closer to the window and sitting down with his puzzle book. He must try to discourage Kay Ormsby. She must be made to realize that there was no chance whatsoever of nuptials. She should get such an idea out of her head, and smartly too. Mr. Wilkie uttered a bark of laughter. He and Kay Ormsby! The notion was ludicrous. But it looked like being a job of work to discourage her, for she had obviously set her cap for him.

FOUR

"Now what seems to be the trouble today, Mrs. Lucas?" asked Mrs. Rawlings, offering a counterfeit smile from behind her outsized tea mug. The two women were in Mrs. Rawlings's office, and Mrs. Lucas had arranged herself into a comfortable position on the small divan beneath the window by the rubber plant. The cars along Transit Road passed to and fro behind her head. She appeared to be settled in for a visit, and Mrs. Rawlings felt a surge of irritation looking at the fat old woman. There was plenty to do this morning and now she was hampered by the presence of Mrs. Lucas, who, the superintendent decided, had the most disagreeable face of any human she had encountered in twenty-five years of senior citizen care. Mrs. Rawlings took a draught of tea from her great mug and listened.

"I have reason to believe," said Mrs. Lucas, "that my new neighbour is not quite sane. Last night I heard the strangest sounds. It was a kind of chant."

"Indeed!" said Mrs. Rawlings. "This is certainly a revelation. Would you care to be more specific, Mrs. Lucas?"

"I could not make out the words," said Mrs. Lucas, staring down at her plump spotted hands. They were

smoothing out the wrinkles in her dress. She looked, Mrs.
Rawlings thought, absurdly pleased with herself.

"She plays strange music too," said Mrs. Lucas. "I had
to tell her to turn down her phonograph. I don't like to be
bad neighbours with people, Mrs. Rawlings, but I can't be
expected to put up with loud music and chanting in the
night. I could hardly sleep at all. I kept thinking that
perhaps she belongs to some cult."

"Some cult, Mrs. Lucas?" Mrs. Rawlings's wiry eyebrows
were now upraised in an attitude of wonderment.

"Why yes," continued Mrs. Lucas. "I was reading a
piece in the *Enquirer* only the other day. It's not only young
people who become members of cults, you know. There
are people in places like Sunset Manor too."

Mrs. Rawlings felt the most overpowering urge to
strike her visitor: to shake her until the glinting spectacles
fell away and the dentures were crushed underfoot by
Mrs. Rawlings's white hospital shoes. It was perhaps time
for another session of primal screaming, a form of therapy
that Mrs. Rawlings had once scoffed at, but now fervently
believed in. If the weather held, she would try to get away
to the woods later in the afternoon.

"Come, come, Mrs. Lucas," said the superintendent,
forcing herself to smile. "This is unlikely. You surely
exaggerate. First it was Mr. Truscott who was a nuisance,
and now it is your new neighbour who has hardly settled
in."

"I only tell you what I heard," said Mrs. Lucas, who sat
on the divan with her hands now still in her lap. She
looked determined and unforgiving. "I pay my account,"
she said. "I have a right to peace and quiet."

"Of course you do," said Mrs. Rawlings. "Indeed you
do. No one in fairness could deny you that. But this all
strikes me as rather strange. I put Miss Ormsby on the
other side of you because she is a cultivated lady. She
taught high school in this town for forty years. Good

heavens above! Chants, you say? This is a woman who until very recently spent an evening a week reading great works of literature to the *blind*. For years she was a member of the Community Concert Board. It's all on her application in black and white. I suggest, Mrs. Lucas, that you are considerably wide of the mark with this talk of chants and cults."

"She smokes too," said Mrs. Lucas. "When I went to tell her to turn her music down, I smelled cigarette smoke from her room."

"It is not forbidden for residents to smoke in their units," said Mrs. Rawlings. "We discourage it, of course, but we do not forbid it. This is not Nazi Germany, Mrs. Lucas."

"I won't be able to sleep for fear of fire."

"I have warned Miss Ormsby of the dangers of smoking on the premises and of the need to be careful. I suggest to you that your fears are groundless."

Mrs. Lucas leaned forward. "I suppose she is a very nice woman, but I must have my sleep, Mrs. Rawlings. If I don't have my sleep, I am all nerves."

Mrs. Rawlings drummed large fingers along the top of her desk. "Perhaps we can help you there, Mrs. Lucas. We have medication in the infirmary for such disorders. Nurse Haines can give you a tablet to help you sleep."

Mrs. Lucas set her jaw firmly, before again pushing her dreadful face forward. "I don't like taking all that dope. It makes me feel funny the next day."

Mrs. Rawlings would have enjoyed marching across the room, kneeling on the old woman's stomach, and prying her jaws open to pour a cupful of sleeping tablets down her throat. It was, she realized, an unworthy fantasy, but powerful for all of that. Some of them, in any case, would be better off asleep. Away from the burdens and cares of this life. Some, of course, took age in their stride. The Huddles and Fenertys of this world were a joy to comfort in their final years. And then there were others, like Mrs. Lucas, for whom nothing was ever right: life was a ledger of complaints and woes. One needed the patience of an ox and the strength of a lion to deal with them.

Mrs. Rawlings smiled again. "Dear Mrs. Lucas. Compromises have to be made. Sunset Manor is a community based on compromise and shared living. We cater to privacy and emphasize the individual. Yet there is room for a fully planned menu of group activities." The familiar words were as soothing as a mantra to Mrs. Rawlings, who had in fact composed them for the institution's promotional literature. Their vagueness seemed to have a calming effect on Mrs. Lucas too. She no longer looked so adamant; instead tears stood out in her eyes. "I have to deal with Mr. Truscott on the other side," she said.

"Now, now, Mrs. Lucas," said Mrs. Rawlings. "Let us hear no more today of Mr. Truscott. That is very old news indeed. Today we are dealing with new problems. Or so it would appear."

"When I'm in the bathroom," said Mrs. Lucas, "he pounds on my wall and says things."

"So you allege, and I have spoken to him about it. Mr. Truscott, however, emphatically denies the accusation."

"He is a liar."

"Harsh words, Mrs. Lucas. And words, I might add, that have no place in our community."

"You could come and listen for yourself."

Mrs. Rawlings looked mildly appalled. "I? Come to your bathroom and listen? That, if I may say so, is an absurd suggestion."

Mrs. Lucas's lower lip had begun to waver. "He does too. And he ordered all those things that were brought to me. He made my life miserable. I never knew what to expect from day to day."

"Perhaps he did," said Mrs. Rawlings, "but nothing was

proven. You must admit, Mrs. Lucas, that it was careless of you to leave your credit card in the Sun Room."

"I was showing it to Mrs. Huddle. She didn't believe that Ward gave me American Express last Christmas."

"We've been through this, Mrs. Lucas. Many many times indeed."

"I forgot it in the Sun Room. That could happen to anyone. Haven't you ever mislaid something, Mrs. Rawlings?"

"Now, Mrs. Lucas . . ."

"He picked it up. He's a thief too."

"Come, come, Mrs. Lucas."

Mrs. Lucas had now begun to cry in earnest. "He makes my life miserable. He should be in an insane asylum. He's not right in the head. We are all in danger." She looked, Mrs. Rawlings thought, like a heavy stupid child in her print dress with the tears rolling down her fleshy cheeks. Sighing, Mrs. Rawlings got to her feet and made her ponderous way around the desk to the divan and the weeping woman. "There, there now, Mrs. Lucas," she said. "We all have our little differences with one another. We must learn to live with them." She applied the flat of her hand to Mrs. Lucas's rounded back. The flesh felt as solid as iron. Mrs. Rawlings gave the rounded back three solid pats. "Why don't you go and watch some television in the Sun Room?"

"Why couldn't I have had the room you gave to the lady with the orange hair?" asked Mrs. Lucas.

"Miss Ormsby's room?" said Mrs. Rawlings. "We can't have people shifting about like Arabs, Mrs. Lucas. Everyone would want to move on a whim. Surely you can see that. One unit is as good as another. Now I will speak again to Mr. Truscott, and I shall have a word with Miss Ormsby about her music and these sounds in the night. She may well indeed have been talking in her sleep. That sometimes happens when people take up new lodgings. She'll get over it, I'm sure. Now how is that, Mrs. Lucas?"

Mrs. Lucas offered up her tearful sullen face and nodded. "Splendid!" said Mrs. Rawlings, moving briskly to her desk and a small tin box. "Have a toffee, Mrs. Lucas! They're from England." Sometimes the old parties liked a boiled candy wrapped up in coloured paper. It reminded them of their childhood. "And now if you'll excuse me," said Mrs. Rawlings, escorting the old woman out of the office. "I, as the poet said, have miles to go before I sleep. And I shall look into your little difficulties. You may rest assured of that." In fact she had no intention of pursuing the matter any further. With a moderate amount of luck, these complaints would eventually force Lucas to seek accommodation elsewhere. She had been a sizeable cross now for three years. There was a waiting list, and surely there was someone on it less demanding and woebegone.

M iss Ormsby sat by the window overlooking the parking lot, watching the snow fall. The large flakes settled over the pavement and on the roofs of the cars. As a child she had enjoyed the snow. Sometimes, as she had walked through a snowfall, she had opened her mouth to taste this freshness from the sky. In later years she nearly always took a walk during the first snow. It was agreeable to be cold and wet and then to come in and be warm and dry. And this snow now covering the gray pavement still lifted her heart, though she was moved to wonder where people walked in this neighbourhood. There were so many cars about. Transit Road always seemed so busy and people were always in a hurry. They drove their cars as though enraged by life itself. Already Miss Ormsby missed Park Street with its tall bare trees and the broad lawns now filling up with snow.

Still there was no point in being downcast. She would

get a bus schedule and find out how to get about the town. There was the library to visit. There were plays and musicals to see at the high school. She liked to keep in touch even if she no longer knew anyone there. There was the liquor store, of course, and the music store. And the cemetery. Even in winter she liked to walk among the trees and stones, and stand before the graves of her mother and father and Addie Bales and others who had gone beyond. It did no harm to be reminded of our brief and mortal span.

Meantime, however, there was life to be lived. Miss Ormsby had put on a favourite recording of Yehudi Menuhin and his son playing Beethoven's *Spring Sonata*. The music was as delicate as a filigree, and its airy lightness gladdened Miss Ormsby's heart. The great man had written the piece when he was thirty and beginning to lose his hearing. In another few months he would be as deaf as wood. What a tragedy! And yet his genius had turned it into a victory for mankind! Could one ever be grateful enough to such men for the gifts they bestowed? "I think not," said Miss Ormsby aloud as she listened to the music and watched the snow.

She was thinking too about her home on Park Street. Yesterday she had walked through the empty house for the last time. She had stood for a moment in the big walk-in closet of her parents' bedroom. Seventy years ago it had been a special room for her; there she had played with her dolls among her mother's dresses and her father's shirts. The place still smelled faintly of her father's clothes but now contained only a half dozen wooden hangers. There was still the same old-fashioned slender light bulb, now a collector's piece no doubt. The auctioneer had somehow missed it. One could still see the filaments through the clear glass. It had hardly been used over the decades.

Miss Ormsby had then gone outside and walked about

the yard in the mild gray afternoon. She had gone down the driveway to the old wooden garage that had leaned to one side for years as though tired. The garage really was a sight, and she had been meaning to do something about it since time out of mind. No wonder the new owners were going to get rid of it. The two front doors were warped by the weather and didn't close properly. It hadn't taken the Dorseys (there, she could remember their names after all) long to decide its fate as they walked around the place with the real estate man. Miss Ormsby had watched from the kitchen and overheard. "That," said the woman, pointing to the old garage, "will have to go. We'll have to get rid of that thing." And her husband kept saying, "No problem, no problem."

But yesterday Miss Ormsby had drawn the rusty bolt from the hasp and with an effort had swung back one of the heavy doors. Pale light flooded over the stained dirt floor. The garage smelled of old wood and dust and motor oil, odours pleasing to Miss Ormsby, who stood in this gloomy winter air breathing deeply. Along the walls were licence plates dating back to 1917. In the rear of the garage was a little workshop where her father had tinkered with things. Miss Ormsby had gone along in there. Everything, of course, had been sold at the auction, and so on the workbench there remained only a few washers, a broken screwdriver, a piece of pipe, a rusty file. Odds and ends from another time.

A strange peace had descended on Miss Ormsby as she stood there staring out the little cobwebbed window that overlooked the raspberry canes. Their privy had once stood in a corner of the yard. Her father had planted lilac bushes by its entrance. Beyond the raspberry canes there used to be an unpainted board fence, and on summer mornings you could see Austin Hewlett's broad straw hat as he worked in his garden. Now and then the straw hat would disappear as the old man stooped to pluck a weed from his corn or beans. The board fence was long gone, replaced by a chain link affair that admitted the sight of a large tub-shaped swimming pool in the backyard opposite.

The Hewlett's had a daughter who was simple, as they used to say. Lillian Hewlett! Miss Ormsby hadn't thought of Lillian Hewlett in years, and yet as a child Miss Ormsby had been terrified of her. Lillian stayed at home until the old people could no longer handle her. She was a big strong girl and used to hit her mother. Miss Ormsby could remember the old woman's cries as they came across the board fence. "Now please, Lilly, please! Be a nice girl, Lilly!" At the supper table Miss Ormsby's mother would shake her head. "That poor woman!" And Miss Ormsby's father, tall and ramrod straight, would drink his tea and say, "It's a shame, but it's not our business, Mary."

One summer morning Miss Ormsby watched through a knothole in the board fence as Lillian Hewlett squatted in the beans to make her water. When the girl stood up, her dress of purple and white polka dots was still above her midriff, and shamefaced, Miss Ormsby glimpsed the girl's dark privates. They finally put Lillian away in the Asylum, and in the dusk of summer evenings, while the swallows and purple martins swooped through the darkening air, old Mrs. Hewlett sat on the back stoop and cried for her mad daughter.

Sitting by the window in Sunset Manor, Miss Ormsby smoked a cigarette and listened to the *Spring Sonata*, watching the snow thicken on the roofs of the cars in the parking lot, remembering the board fence and the raspberry canes and another summer morning when she was twelve. There was a family gathering that day. Uncle Everett and Uncle Will had come from their farms, and Uncle Charlie had driven up from Toronto in his new Durrant motor car. In the kitchen Miss Ormsby's large amiable aunts helped her mother prepare the dinner. Miss Ormsby's cousins, large shy youngsters who smelled of farm animals and looked flushed and clumsy in their Sunday clothes, seemed dumbfounded to find themselves in town. In a few hours they would be back at their tasks in the barn and the fields. Now they walked through the house or hung about the wide verandah listening to their fathers and uncles talk.

Handsome Uncle Will, the youngest of the four brothers, was Miss Ormsby's favourite; he'd been in the Great War and had seen England and France and Belgium. On that summer morning he leaned into the soft green leaves of Dutchman's Pipe that covered the verandah, laughing shyly at his older brothers' stories. He would die the following summer, felled by a bolt of lightning as he crossed a field of barley to get out of the rain. Miss Ormsby's father was the eldest, and he sat on a wicker chair smoking his pipe and nodding at the talk of weather and crops. He had left the farm behind him, but he still liked to hear country talk. Uncle Everett, a slow, kind, and ponderous man, sat on the steps, leaning his broad back against the verandah railing as he talked. Uncle Charlie, who had gone to the city and found a job driving a streetcar, paced back and forth. He was a restless and impatient man who thought himself sharper than his country brothers. He looked like a bit of a dandy in his brown and yellow checked suit that was belted at the back. He had a watch fob and chain and smoked tailor-made cigarettes and winked at Miss Ormsby. He was supposed to be up to his ears in debt. To the discomfort of his brothers he liked to describe the pretty women who got on his trolly car. There was always an air of lewdness surrounding Uncle Charlie.

He had just married Aunt Mildred, a shy, pretty woman who was several years younger, and their baby Marion was only a few months old. The child was still something of a novelty, and Aunt Mildred played with her as a youngster might play with a doll. Miss Ormsby's mother and aunts fussed over the baby and asked Miss Ormsby if she wanted to hold her, but she said no. The baby, suffering with prickly heat, cried a great deal, and Miss Ormsby didn't feel at ease holding her. She had looked down at the tiny wrinkled sobbing face and fled to the garden.

Stepping around the tomatoes and peas she walked behind the garage to stand among the raspberry canes, a lanky awkward girl. From the garden she could faintly hear the cries of the child and the piercing shrieks of the cicadas high in the oaks and maples along Park Street. There was poetry in this summer morning of drowsy heat with its smell of the board fence and the raspberries. Then Uncle Charlie came out of the privy buttoning his trousers. He had taken off his suit coat and now stood there looking at her. There were sleeve gaiters on his striped shirt. Uncle Charlie appraised her as she stood among the hot raspberry bushes. The air seemed to shimmer with heat as he stepped forward and placed his large pale hands upon her shoulders. He was smiling. "Why Kay," he said. "You're getting so big. I'd say you're going to be a tall girl. Just like the Ormsbys, eh! I wonder just how tall. Let's see now." And grasping her shoulders he pressed her thin dress against his body. She was startled by the gesture, for the Ormsbys were not a touching family. In all her years she had never seen her parents embrace. And now she felt her uncle next to her, smelled the cigarette smoke and bay rum on him, and felt the texture of his trousers against her bare legs.

Uncle Charlie placed the palm of his hand on the top of her head as he measured her height against his chest. "Yes sir!" he said. "You're getting to be a big girl, as sure as candy. And I'll bet you've got a funny bone too." To her astonishment, her uncle began to tickle her. "Yes sir, yes sir," he kept saying as he touched her. She could feel his hands through the thin dress. "Yes, quite a young lady now," he whispered. How strong he was, she thought. And then it was over and he held her at arms' length. He was panting a little, and his face was ruddy in the strong August sunlight. They could hear the baby crying. Uncle Charlie fumbled for a coin in his change purse, a little black leather bag with a clasp. He placed a nickel in her palm. "You're a good girl, Kay," he said. "Now you can get yourself some ice cream." With a wink he left her standing among the raspberry canes listening to the cicadas and the crying child.

In the chair by the window Miss Ormsby felt a mild flutter of panic. For a moment she had forgotten where she was. Her cigarette had burned away in the pipe ashtray. She had been recalling a summer morning in 1926. That was ages ago! And Uncle Charlie and Aunt Mildred and even her cousin Marion, who had been a tiny sobbing baby that day, were now gone from this earth. The Beethoven recording was over and Miss Ormsby could hear her neighbour coughing. Today she would try to discover the woman's name.

FIVE

"How are they hangin', Cleggy?" asked Lorne Truscott. He was standing in the hallway on the main floor by the telephone booth. Stooped and frail Mr. Clegg was making his cautious way to the Sun Room, shuffling along in his plaid bedroom slippers, holding on to the wall with his right hand for support. Never a robust man, he had nevertheless survived nine decades, though the years had bent him finally into the shape of a large question mark. At Lorne Truscott's query the old man stopped, and because of the stiffness in his various parts, turned ninety degrees to his left, peering through cataracts at a gray shadowy figure. "What was that?" he asked in a voice so high and thin that it might have been piped through a keyhole. Lorne waved the old fellow away and stepped into the phone booth to dial his granddaughter's number. Mr. Clegg turned ninety degrees to the right and proceeded on his course, uncertain in fact as to whether he had been addressed at all. He thought no more about it, however, for confusion ruled his every waking hour.

In the booth Lorne Truscott waited for someone to answer the phone. The pain in his arse this morning was fierce and unrelenting. He had awakened with it, imagining a red hot poker shoved up there and twisted by some fiend from hell. A woman with a nest of rollers on her head walked by the booth, and Lorne slammed a fist against the glass and shouted, "Why don't you fix your goddamn hair before appearing in public?" Either the woman didn't hear this muffled outburst or she chose to ignore it. Lorne heard a small voice at the end of the line. "Who is that?" he asked.

"Jason Kevin Truscott," said the voice.

Lorne laughed. "Jason Kevin Truscott! What a handle! Do you know who this is?"

"Yes. It's Great-gramps. Do you have any candy for me, Great-gramps?"

"I got lots of candy. I'm eatin' candy right now. You come and see me on Sunday and I'll give you some. How's your sister?"

The child ignored his question. "I got a new truck. Randy bought it for me."

"Who the hell is Randy?" asked Lorne.

"My Mom's friend."

Lorne rubbed his whiskers. "Another one! Jesus! What happened to Wayne?"

"My Mom don't like him anymore. They had a fight. The police were here. The light on the top of their car was going around."

"Is that right? When was that Jason?"

"Last Saturday I think."

"Let me talk to your mother."

"She's in bed. We were up late watching movies. We got a whole bunch of videos, Great-gramps."

"Say . . . why aren't you in school today?"

"I don't have to go. School's out for Christmas. Anyway it's Saturday. What are you going to get me for Christmas, Great-gramps?"

"I ain't decided yet. You ain't gettin' nothin' if you don't come to see me on Sunday, you little bugger."

"Hello, Great-gramps," said another little voice.

"Is that my Becky?"

"Mommy's got a new friend, Great-gramps. He's sleeping in her bed now. He's got a black truck. He bought me a doll house."

"Is that right?"

Lorne heard his granddaughter shooing away the kids. When she spoke to him, her voice was full of sleep. "Hullo, Gramps."

"You comin' to see me tomorrow, Rhonda?" he asked.

He heard her yawn. "Yeh. Randy's going to drive us."

Lorne grunted. "You had some trouble with the other one? Is that it?"

"That asshole. He should be locked up. He's crazy."

"Is this new one any better then?"

"Randy's okay, Gramps."

"What's he work at?"

"He's between jobs right now. He's got his own truck. He hauls stuff."

Lorne heard his granddaughter yelling at the kids. It had something to do with the television. "I got to go, Gramps. I'll see you on Sunday. I'll bring the kids."

"You do that, Rhonda. And take care."

"You too, Gramps."

Lorne hung up the phone. The fiend was giving the poker a few more rotations. Lorne decided to go to his room and lie down for a spell.

Mrs. Lucas sat in her rocking chair reading material from the *Call of Tomorrow* people. They had sent her numerous pamphlets and a handsome calendar upon which were written passages of Scripture for every day of the year. Today's verse was from the *Gospel According to Mark*, Chapter 10, Verse 13. "Except ye be converted and become as little children, ye shall not enter into the Kingdom of Heaven." Mrs. Lucas rocked in her chair and pondered these words. She was sure that they didn't mean that everyone who was going to Heaven would have to become a little child again. How could you do that? It made no sense at all. What they probably meant was that a person had to become like a little child *in spirit*.

In Mrs. Lucas's cedar chest were boxes of pictures, and there was a photograph of her as a child. In the picture she wore a white dress and stockings and black shoes. Her hair was done up in sausage curls with a ribbon and bow. She had been a plump and pretty child. Mrs. Lucas could remember the day that picture was taken. It was a Sunday morning before church and her father had taken the picture by the side of the house on Argyle Street. He took pictures of her brothers and sisters too, but he took this one especially for her, and then they all went to church.

That photograph was in an old Laura Secord box in the cedar chest, but Mrs. Lucas seldom took out her pictures anymore. The truth of the matter was that it was too sad to look at pictures of people and scenes that could never be again. There were hundreds of photographs in the chocolate boxes in the cedar chest, but Mrs. Lucas had decided that she was finished with them. It was all wrong to take photographs, and if she had her way, no pictures would ever be taken. It just made you too sad to look at them.

Her son, Ward, was always taking pictures. Pictures of the children and pictures of Irma and pictures of holidays they'd taken. He brought them over to show her on Sunday afternoons. But what good did taking all those pictures do you? Sooner or later they all ended up in chocolate boxes in your cedar chest, and when you took them out and looked at them and saw how the past got swallowed up and people you once knew had now passed away, it just broke your heart. Mrs. Lucas felt her eyes brimming with tears. Life was certainly unfair in that respect.

She used the hem of her dress to wipe her glasses and again read the words about entering the Kingdom of Heaven as a little child. She could write Pastor Bob and ask him to explain just what was meant by the passage. Her question might even be asked on the program, in which case she would receive a special prayer. Pastor Bob invited members of his audience to write in with their questions. If she could find the paper and an envelope, she supposed she might do it, though it seemed like a lot of work and she doubted whether she had any envelopes.

Mrs. Lucas listened to her stomach making noises. She was hungry and wondered what was on for lunch. She couldn't remember the announcement. In another couple of days she would go to Ward's for Christmas dinner. Irma put up a good meal, she had to admit that. There would be roast turkey and stuffing and potatoes and bread and butter pickles. Mincemeat pies. Irma's pies had a good flaky crust. She could put together a solid Christmas dinner, all right; there was no question about that. But Ward was putting on weight. Mrs. Lucas had noticed it during his last visit. Ward, she decided, had better watch his heart. His own father had been carried off in his sixties. And Ward was now what? Fifty-seven! It still amazed Mrs. Lucas that she should have a son now in his late fifties. It hardly seemed possible, yet there it was. When Ward came to see her on Sunday afternoons, she was astonished each time at the sight of him. With Joan it was different. Her daughter had lived in Vancouver for years and Mrs. Lucas seldom saw her. In Mrs. Lucas's estimation, Joan was still the sharp-tongued and troublesome girl she had always been. Even her voice sounded the same on the telephone.

Mrs. Lucas could hear stirring in the next room; it sounded like someone shifting about. Old Truscott was quiet this morning, but the woman with the orange hair was moving about. Earlier she had played her music, but not as loud as the night before, and that was thoughtful of her. Maybe Mrs. Rawlings had talked to her. Or maybe she was just a very nice person. Underneath it all people could be very nice, Mrs. Lucas decided. After all, you had to live and let live. Mrs. Lucas felt suddenly overcome by a suffusion of goodwill towards her neighbour. Perhaps they could become real friends. She could be lonely just like me, thought Mrs. Lucas. Whether you had children or not didn't matter in the end because they cast you aside and got on with their own lives and where did that leave you? It left you to make do with people your own age, that's where it left you. Maybe, thought Mrs. Lucas, she could borrow an envelope from her neighbour and write to Pastor Bob about the little children entering Heaven. When she went for the envelope, she might take along some of the literature and talk about the *Call of Tomorrow* program. She might even win a disciple for Christ. If the woman with the orange hair signed the tally sheet, Mrs. Lucas would receive a scroll with her name on it and a recording of a hymn sung by the *Call of Tomorrow* songsters.

The scrolls were very attractive. They were displayed on the program by Pastor Bob's assistants, nice young men and women in powder blue jackets. If you signed ten sinners, you were invited to spend a weekend with all expenses paid at Pastor Bob's ranch in California, where there was a frontier village of the Old West. You also got a tour through Pastor Bob's ranch house, where there were gold faucets on the bathroom fixtures. Mrs. Lucas had seen it on the television. It was certainly something to think about.

Mrs. Lucas tried to ignore the sounds from her empty stomach. They didn't feed you half enough in the place. Mrs. Rawlings had said that the woman with the orange hair was a school teacher, and on reflection that put a different colouring on things. In Mrs. Lucas's opinion school teachers thought themselves pretty high and mighty, and over the years Mrs. Lucas had had her share of trouble with them. She could remember Joan coming home from the high school in tears after failing some test. A child of fourteen and dissolved into tears because of some foolish test! Where was the sense in it? Mrs. Lucas could remember it as if it were yesterday. It was late winter, March probably, because the streets were slushy. She had put on her coat and galoshes and marched through the wet streets to the high school to give them a piece of her mind. Someone had to do it, and certainly George had never been one to face things like that. George would never stand up to anybody; it was always left to her. So she had marched right into that teacher's classroom after school, and she had told him a thing or two about making fourteen-year-old girls cry over some silly test. She could remember telling Joan's teacher that, at that very moment, her daughter was home lying on her bed and crying her eyes out. And why? Because of a test. The teacher had backed right down, too. He said he would allow Joan to write the test again, and she did, and she passed.

Maybe, however, she wouldn't have if Mrs. Lucas hadn't gone up to the high school and stood up for her. That was the whole thing in a nutshell; you had to stand up for yourself and your children. Teachers would just take advantage of you if you let them. They weren't half as smart as they let on. Mrs. Lucas was now rocking quite fast as she thought about the incident with her daughter and the failed test. As she rocked vigorously back and forth, she allowed that her goodwill towards her neighbour had dissipated, and that in fact she was now bristling with indignation. Mrs. Lucas decided that she would wait until she was in a calmer state of mind before paying a visit.

Miss Ormsby was dressed for the weather in an old cloth coat with a heavy woollen scarf cast about her throat in the fashion of European students. She also wore leather mittens and a beret that looked something like a large green pie plate. On her feet were old-style fur-topped boots. Mrs. Rawlings, who had just emerged from her office, hadn't seen such footwear in forty years. Miss Ormsby was standing by the front door pulling on her mittens.

"My dear Miss Ormsby," said Mrs. Rawlings. "You are surely not going outdoors in such weather?"

"I am indeed, Mrs. Rawlings," said Miss Ormsby. "As the state of my dress would indicate." She cocked her head to one side and frowned.

"Can something not be done about this music, Mrs. Rawlings? Surely the residents can't enjoy listening to this Jingle Bell nonsense all the time?"

Mrs. Rawlings was certain that she could smell drink on Miss Ormsby, and it wasn't yet noon. And now the woman was going out into a snowstorm! What next?

"But the weather, Miss Ormsby," said Mrs. Rawlings. "It's storming."

"I love to walk in the snow," Miss Ormsby said. "And then I enjoy coming back into the warmth. I find the contrast extremely satisfying."

"This is not the centre of town, Miss Ormsby. Transit Road is a busy artery. I fear for your safety."

"Thank you for your concern, Mrs. Rawlings," said Miss Ormsby, "but I shall be careful. I shall cross at the light and walk around the shopping mall. It's not perfect, but it's better than nothing. I have walked two miles every day of my life for as long as I can remember."

"But Miss Ormsby," said Mrs. Rawlings. "There is no need to risk life and limb out of doors. We have every athletic facility in our gymnasium. We have walking boards with dials that measure the distance travelled."

"I have no wish to walk on a treadmill, Mrs. Rawlings."

Mrs. Rawlings smiled with hatred at the tall foolishly

dressed woman who was displaying unmistakable signs of being a troublemaker.

"You may of course do as you wish, Miss Ormsby, but I advise against it. The streets have not yet been salted. You could take a fall."

"I could take a fall on your stairs, Mrs. Rawlings. We mustn't be timid over what might happen." Miss Ormsby made a face as she listened to "Silent Night."

"It's hard to believe that people enjoy a steady diet of that stuff, Mrs. Rawlings."

"Stuff, Miss Ormsby?"

"Yes. The so-called music that is piped through the halls all day long. Christmas music can be very beautiful of course. One thinks of Bach's oratorios or the great *Messiah*. But even great music can become tiresome through over-exposure. Not to mention this jingle jangle stuff. I find it difficult to believe that people would welcome such intrusions into their thoughts."

Mrs. Rawlings again smiled. "Ah, that is where you are very wrong, Miss Ormsby. The residents enjoy the music."

Miss Ormsby looked thoughtful. "Are you sure about that? Have you done a survey of any kind? It would certainly be interesting to know the results."

Mrs. Rawlings gave a short bitter laugh. "I do not think a survey is necessary, Miss Ormsby. Sunset Manor is a community, and we who have been here for some considerable time know what's best for everyone. You'll forgive me, I'm sure, if I suggest that you should perhaps wait until you have lived here a little longer and become acquainted with our lifestyle before you jump to conclusions about what other people like or dislike. As for our music, most residents find that it is relaxing and indeed inspiring."

Miss Ormsby was looking out the glass door towards the snow. She seemed lost in thought. "I wonder," she said at last before opening the door. "Goodbye, Mrs. Rawlings."

Mrs. Rawlings watched Miss Ormsby walk across the parking lot in the swirling snow towards the traffic lights. The woman had definitely been drinking and from the sound of her was already mildly intoxicated. She could prove to be a handful. A drinker who also smoked spelled trouble on the premises. There had once been a Miss Phelan who drank table wine and set her bed on fire. Miss Ormsby would certainly bear scrutiny, and a peek at her unit was most assuredly in order. With this in mind Mrs. Rawlings ascended the stairs to the second floor.

The hallway was empty at this hour; most of the residents were in the Sun Room or gymnasium. Others were at their morning classes of yoga or landscape painting. Mrs. Rawlings could hear the roar of a vacuum cleaner from a room down the hall. Otherwise there seemed to be no one about. However, as Mrs. Rawlings inserted her master key into the lock of Miss Ormsby's door, Mrs. Lucas came out of her room and stood there looking at the administrator. "The new lady has gone out," said Mrs. Lucas. "She left five minutes ago."

"I am aware of that, Mrs. Lucas," said Mrs. Rawlings. "This is a security check I am conducting."

Mrs. Lucas did not look convinced. "Have you talked to her about the music?"

"Things are well in hand, Mrs. Lucas. You mustn't fret."

"She smokes cigarettes."

"I am aware of that. And now if you'll excuse me," said Mrs. Rawlings, opening the door and letting herself in.

That horrid Lucas woman was always underfoot, thought Mrs. Rawlings as she looked around Miss Ormsby's unit. Mrs. Rawlings liked to get a handle on new residents; she liked to see where their interests lay. You could tell a good deal about a person by acquainting yourself with her personal effects. How she arranged her belongings provided an essential clue to understanding

71

her disposition. Mrs. Rawlings sniffed the stale smoky air. The housekeeper had made the bed and tidied up what she could, but the place was still in disarray because of the books. There were books everywhere. The taxi driver had wrestled several boxes and cases into the elevator before the woman had even arrived. Mrs. Rawlings enjoyed reading a book now and again, but surely one could have too much of a good thing.

There was also a large phonograph and stacks of records. On a small table near the bed stood a glass and a bottle of Johnny Walker. Well she certainly didn't bother to hide it, thought Mrs. Rawlings. Many of the residents dressed up their units with religious calendars and cushions and pillows embroidered with messages of inspiration. Mrs. Rawlings approved of and encouraged such decoration. It made the atmosphere more homey, and then religion was a great consolation in one's senior years.

Miss Ormsby, however, had none of this. On the dresser was a single photograph: an old black and white picture of a tall man and his short wife. They stood unsmiling by the side of a brick house. They were doubtless the parents: simple country folk who looked uneasy in front of a camera. The picture must have been taken ages ago. Mrs. Rawlings opened the drawers of the dresser and carefully inspected the stockings and scarves and bloomers. The latter appeared to be unstained. At least she was continent and that was a blessing.

On the little table next to the whiskey bottle was an old book with a leather cover and a ribbon page marker. On the fly leaf were the words *To Kay. Happy Christmas. Mother. Christmas 1929*. Mrs. Rawlings turned to the title page. *Nicholas Nickleby* by Charles Dickens. What peculiar old-fashioned taste the woman had!

In the hallway Mrs. Lucas stood by the elevator. She was en route to the Sun Room to wait out the half hour before lunch. As she entered the empty elevator she repeated for perhaps the tenth time, "Security check, my eye."

SIX

The gymnasium was festooned with streamers and coloured lights; big straw hats had been pinned to the walls to suggest the motif of fiesta time in old Mexico. The maintenance people had rigged up a large revolving light on the ceiling, and as it slowly turned and cast its beams across the floor, one might have imagined a resort ballroom circa 1943. The more nimble residents of Sunset Manor shuffled about in stockinged feet while others observed from chairs lined up against the walls. The oldest and most infirm had also arranged their walking frames and wheelchairs along the sidelines.

At a table near the weight room, Mr. Neil Kenny, a retired druggist and the evening's disc jockey, watched over his spinning records, introducing each song with an amiable manner remembered from fifty years ago when he had listened to radio announcers introducing big band music from hotel ballrooms in Chicago and New York. The foxtrot was the order of the evening, but there were also sprightly Latin tunes to set the heart's blood singing; at one point, a rhumba line had been attempted. A few adventurous couples were now maneuvering their way through a slow jive accompanied by Glen Miller's "Chattanooga Choo-Choo." Mrs. Rawlings and Nurse Haines kept an eye on them; one couldn't be too careful. At the Harvest Ball, Mr. Ripley, an octogenarian, had taken a tumble while doing the Chicken Dance. The old man had fallen on his elbow and cracked the bone.

The music brought back memories to many of the residents of Sunset Manor: memories of wartime dances and the feel of khaki tunics against cheeks and the smell of cigarette smoke; memories of rides in solid old Plymouths and Fords down from the Parkview Pavilion to the edge of the dark lake and the lighted dials of car radios and the eager rough hands on garter belts; memories of lemon gin and coke and the fumbling with Trojans and the lovely, lovely music from cities far away.

Throughout the Manor the music could be faintly heard, a distant sound to those who were already preparing for bed with cups of Ovaltine to aid sleep or hot water to unplug bowels. Sleeping tablets were washed down and old bones eased under covers. Mrs. Fenerty was already asleep. In another few hours she would awaken and stare into the darkness, remembering a time when there were no automobiles or airplanes or radios, when streets were muddy in spring and children died of diphtheria or consumption as had her poor brother Tommy.

Mr. Wilkie had removed his hearing aid and lay abed in pyjamas of white and blue stripes. He had no wish to hear the dance music. At dances women approached you and became familiar; they pressed themselves against you and the next thing you knew, they were asking about the state of your annuities and RSP's. They wanted to know whether you still owned your house and were renting it as income property. He had never been one for dancing anyway; his long, ungainly legs had never mastered the steps. Ada was the same. When they were courting, both preferred the picture shows. After the polio, of course, she was in her chair and that was that. Neither of them missed it.

He used, however, to see a woman named Edith Pollet who was mad for dancing. She was a childless woman whose husband was a captain on a lake freighter. Mr. Wilkie used to visit her on summer afternoons when her husband was out on Lake Superior and Ada was spending a month at her mother's cottage in Muskoka. Edith always wanted to dance before they did it. She had a phonograph in the living room and she would have the thick black discs spinning on the turntable by the time he arrived. She also had the drapes pulled across the living room windows and she liked to dance barefoot in her slip. She said she liked it best when it was dark and thundery outside with the rain streaming against the windows. He had always thought that a queer notion though he never said anything. Just as often, however, it was bright and sunny, though the house was enclosed in shadows as they clasped one another and moved slowly over the living room carpet. She was not a good housekeeper, and after a while the soles of her feet would get dirty. It put him off slightly, those soiled feet.

In many ways she was a careless foolish woman who never got the hang of subterfuge. Sometimes deliverymen came to the door with parcels and receipts to sign. Once they were nearly caught by a neighbour whose child had broken an arm falling from a tree. The neighbour pounded on the door because Edith had a car and it was suggested that she take the child to the hospital. While the neighbour was in the kitchen talking to Edith, Mr. Wilkie had hidden in a bedroom closet waiting for them to go. Edith and her husband eventually moved away to Goderich or Owen Sound or some other town on the lake. She used to like to get on top. She said she preferred it that way.

Mr. Wilkie decided he would try to awaken next morning an hour earlier at five-thirty. That would give him plenty of time to be dressed and ready for the first setting at breakfast. He imagined that Kay Ormsby wouldn't be about that early, and therefore he wouldn't have to endure conversations about what she thought he had said thirty years ago. Mr. Wilkie had turned off all the lights except the night lamp that enabled him to see his way to the bathroom, for he always awoke at three o'clock to empty his bladder.

Mr. Wilkie's long thin hands smoothed out his blanket. Its pattern was yellow and brown parallel lines, and Mr. Wilkie imagined railway tracks spreading through the countryside. He had always used railway tracks as examples of parallel lines; the students could understand that. The parallel lines on his blanket also made him think of railroad journeys he had taken as a child seventy-five years ago. His father was a conductor on the CPR and entitled to a family pass. Each Christmas they travelled to his Uncle Herman's in Winnipeg. Mr. Wilkie could remember the dark red wooden stations and the immense locomotive with steam pouring from it, and the overheated wooden coaches that smelled of hot wet wool and coal smoke. He could remember looking out at the miles of dark trees among the snow and the outcroppings of gray rock. He imagined being lost in the woods and eaten by bears or wolves.

His father knew the men who punched their tickets or made up their berths. Once Mr. Wilkie and his brother were allowed to pass through the swaying coaches, onto the freezing passageways into the empty diner, and finally to the baggage car where men were sorting mail and cooking eggs over a tiny spirit stove. In the middle of the night the train would jolt to a stop, and Mr. Wilkie at the age of ten would awaken and peer through the frosted window of his berth at men pulling iron-wheeled carts loaded with luggage. The men's breath smoked in the yellow light, and by the side of the station, a horse with a blanket across its back stomped a foot.

In the morning the cheerful black porters helped the family with the bags. One of them once gave Mr. Wilkie a tin whistle, a prize from a cereal box. But Mr. Wilkie's mother would not let him blow into it because she was worried that the black man's lips had touched the whistle, so she confiscated it. And Mr. Wilkie had a temper tantrum so intense that his father paddled him with a shoe.

Now, seventy-five years later in his silent world, Mr. Wilkie awaited sleep, turning over in his mind the parallel lines of railway tracks, replacing them with the image of a freighter on the lakes. Perhaps its captain was Edith Pollet's husband. Mr. Wilkie saw the freighter moving through the deep black water of Lake Superior towards a distant lighthouse. Suppose the lighthouse were a hundred feet high, and from its top the freighter is sighted at an angle of depression of forty-seven degrees? How far would the vessel be from the lighthouse? For Mr. Wilkie, problems in trigonometry were always a satisfying prelude to sleep.

In his bed Lorne Truscott watched the snow falling through the dark sky. It had been a bad day, though the whiskey helped, and the pain in his rectum had at last subsided. He could faintly hear the music from the dance. On Friday nights he used to go to the Legion, where they had a little band. Now, however, the place was filled with young people; the Legion wasn't the same anymore. It was filled with young snots who wouldn't talk to you. The last time he was there was months ago, and he got into an argument with some young punk. He couldn't even remember what the argument had been about, but Mortson told him not to come back unless he could drink quietly.

Could you beat that, for Christ's sake? Drink quietly? And he'd been going to the Legion for twenty years! But then he couldn't drink beer anymore anyway. It just went through him like water. And buying whiskey in that place was too goddamn expensive. So to hell with them! He'd have his whiskey right here in his own room and they could all go piss up a rope for all he cared.

Lorne watched the snow storming against the window. Another goddamn winter! How tired he had become of these long winter months! Some of the lucky bastards who had money got to go to Florida. Lorne tried to imagine what it would be like living in Florida in a nice little trailer. Palm trees around you and oranges and hot sunny days. He hated the cold anymore. But if you didn't go out, you had to stay in this goddamn place, surrounded by a lot of old women who wanted you to take fucking rhumba lessons or play bingo. It was a goddamn shame that none of the kids had room for him. But he wasn't going to go on about that. To hell with them too! You had six kids and none of them had room for you. If Billy were still around, thought Lorne, he'd have a place to stay. Billy would have looked after him.

Whenever he thought about his oldest son, Lorne found himself taking quick deep breaths. His son's death was something Lorne couldn't get rid of; it had happened and that was it. You had to live with it for the rest of your life. Cassie had been spared, and Lorne sometimes wondered if she hadn't been lucky; if it weren't better to die before one of your children did. How many times had he warned him not to drink so goddamn much? Coming home from that hotel loaded like that! Lorne quickly drank the rest of his whiskey. It did no fucking good to think about what happened. It happened and that was it. It didn't take Josie long to get married again either. Of course, she was a Lovett and none of them was worth a pinch of coon shit. If Billy hadn't knocked her up, he'd have told him to stay clear of them. Josie was a tramp, no two ways about it. And if it hadn't been for Lorne, Rhonda would have ended up in the Children's Aid. The world was full of assholes. Maybe he hadn't picked up too much in his life, but at least he'd learned that.

Lorne stared at the ceiling and yawned. There was nothing doing next door; the old fartbag must have gone to bed early. Well he'd fix her wagon next week. He still had a thing or two up his sleeve. Turning his head, Lorne again looked out at the falling snow and waited for sleep. Sooner or later it always came.

Mrs. Lucas had been reading an article about aliens in Kansas. Apparently these aliens had taken this couple and held them captive for two hours before letting them go. Mrs. Lucas knew there were people who didn't believe such stories, but who was to say that there weren't such creatures living on other planets? Why shouldn't there be, for goodness sakes? Mrs. Lucas put away the tabloid and dropped a Polident tablet into the glass on the bedside table. She watched the green mixture fizz and foam around her pink dentures.

Settling herself into bed she thought about the forthcoming weekend. Saturdays were always busy in the Manor; people took baths and had their hair fixed for Sunday visitors. Sunday was Mrs. Lucas's favourite day. Ward brought her the new *Enquirer*, and Irma, say what you like about her, brought along cookies or a piece of matrimony cake. The woman had a way with baked goods, though Mrs. Lucas had to watch her sugar intake. On Sunday morning there was the *Call of Tomorrow* program, and this reminded Mrs. Lucas that she should call on her neighbour and ask to borrow an envelope in which to send her question to Pastor Bob, though she couldn't remember just now what the question was. But maybe that didn't matter. Maybe what mattered was visiting her neighbour and making her feel welcome.

That was the trouble nowadays, thought Mrs. Lucas. People weren't neighbourly the way they used to be. In the old days people talked to one another and borrowed this and that when they needed it. People chatted to one another over the backyard fences. When Mrs. Lucas thought about it, however, she had to admit that she'd never had much luck with neighbours. For instance, there were the Mullens, who rented the Pitfield place next to them. It was a nice yellow frame house with a garden, but you never saw a place get so run down so fast. Pat Mullen soon had that yard filled with old cars with no wheels on them. He was forever up to his elbows in grease tinkering with those old cars. He never worked at any job so far as she could discover. One day he took an old tire and he tied it by a rope to a tree branch and the children swung in that thing all summer long. It drove you crazy listening to them, and the little girls wore no underpants. It was a disgrace to the street.

Those Mullen kids, the older ones, were always getting into trouble. Lloyd Mullen used to pick on Ward something awful. Lloyd Mullen was a big homely boy, and he and his brothers used to run around all summer in windbreakers and rubber boots. Then when winter came they were barely dressed; they used to go to school in running shoes in the dead of winter. The Mullens stole from her woodpile at night too; she'd watched them from her bedroom window. George, of course, wouldn't say a thing to them and the police wouldn't do anything about it either. They said they couldn't keep a man watching her woodpile every night of the week. That's how helpful Charley Johnson was when she spoke to him about it. She'd never forgot what he said and wouldn't on her dying day.

The Mullens were a dirty bunch too. The older boys

were always saying things to Joan and one of them even waved his thing at her one day when she was on her way to school; she couldn't have been more than thirteen or fourteen at the time. She just happened to look up at their front bedroom window, and one of the Mullen boys had his business out and was waving it at her. But just try to make Charley Johnson believe that's what happened and see how far you got? He'd rather believe the word of trash like the Mullen boys. He said it couldn't be proven. He wouldn't hear Joan's side of the story at all. One of those Mullen girls married into Truscott's family. Trash marrying trash, no two ways about that!

Mrs. Lucas decided that when she called on her neighbour, she would tell her about Mrs. Rawlings being in her room. Mrs. Rawlings had no call to do that. She shouldn't be going into rooms when people weren't there. Security check she called it. My eye! It wasn't the right thing to do, but it was the same with the housekeepers. Foreigners most of them or Indians. Nice enough, but they liked you out of the way when they cleaned your room. Once Mrs. Lucas lost twenty dollars and she went to Mrs. Rawlings about it. Mrs. Lucas was sure that the Indian girl from Christian Island had taken the money. A number of other people were complaining about things missing: brooches and pins and this and that. There was a fuss made, and eventually Mrs. Rawlings let the Indian girl go. Months later Mrs. Lucas found the twenty-dollar bill between the pages of her Bible where she must have left it as a bookmark. At the time it didn't seem worthwhile telling anybody; after all, the girl had probably stolen money from others.

Lying in bed Mrs. Lucas listened to her stomach rumble. She had taken two spoonfuls of Pepto-Bismol™, but the Shepherd's Pie at supper had been heavily spiced. They couldn't cook worth a pin in that kitchen, but you had to eat what they put in front of you. Mrs. Lucas could just hear the dance music from the gymnasium. She could now scarcely imagine dancing on her swollen mottled feet. Yet she and George used to go dancing at the Orange Hall on Saturday nights.

George was a good dancer. He was light and quick on his feet and she couldn't keep up to him. It was the only time he'd get irritated with her. "Just follow me, Ettie," he used to say, pushing her slow heavy body around the hall. "Watch my feet!" He wore those nice brown and white wing-tipped shoes. George was always a natty dresser when he went out in public. And so she'd watch those brown and white shoes, but all to no avail. She just couldn't follow him, and after a while she'd sit down and have a lime rickey while George danced with others. She just had no sense of rhythm, but you could hardly say it was her fault. You can't do anything about your nature. Ward was like her. As a child he was clumsy. Always bumping into things.

Now Joan was more like her father. She was quick and ran in races at school field days. She was always winning ribbons and bringing them home. And always complaining that her mother never went out to watch her run! But who had time to be traipsing off to school field days? Whenever she thought about her daughter, Mrs. Lucas was bemused. It was strange how they had never seen eye to eye on anything. Joan always went to her father, and of course he always sided with her. George was like that. He was far too lenient with both children. He always left it up to her to do the scolding when it was needed.

Joan was such a headstrong girl. Now she lived on the other side of the country in British Columbia. Mrs. Lucas visited her once. It was the year after George's death and her first time on an airplane. She had so looked forward to that trip, but really, when all was said and done, it was a disappointment. You were cramped up in those narrow seats, and it was hard to eat those little meals with people's

83

elbows in your sides. She had trouble opening those tiny containers of salad dressing and cream. Of course, her fingers were badly swollen. Flying made you swell up; you retained your bodily fluids in the air. She'd read that once.

The trip just wasn't as nice as she thought it would be, and when it came to that, neither was Vancouver. It seemed to rain most of the time. She used to stand by the front window of Joan's little bungalow looking out at the gray sky and the damp lawns. Joan's husband was retired from the Post Office and they just sat around all day watching television. You couldn't get a conversation out of them. Joan had turned awful cranky with the years. So had Ward for that matter, but he wasn't as bad as Joan.

Ward had never been as difficult as his sister. He was such a nice little boy. She could remember him in a sailor suit, and he was as cute as a bug's ear. He was built a little on the chunky side like her. And he never gave her a bit of trouble as a youngster. Now he was growing a little cranky too. Maybe he was passing through the change of life. Mrs. Lucas wondered if men had to go through something like that too. If they did, it couldn't be as bad as what a woman has to endure. She could certainly remember the awful time she had. She used to go through a tin of Instantine™ tablets a week with those headaches. There were so many awful things in life when you thought about it. She'd heard only the other day in the Sun Room that there were now holes in the sky caused by these spray cans. The earth was getting warmer every year.

Mrs. Lucas turned her mind to the alien ships that were written about in her paper. She tried to picture those huge gleaming saucers as they journeyed through space, far above the snow and the clouds, way beyond the reaches of the human eye where stars and planets hung like enormous lamps in the darkness. Beyond that must be Heaven, and perhaps these alien ships travelled from there. In all fairness, who could deny the possibility?

"As Mr. Crummles had a strange four-legged animal in the inn stables, which he called a pony, and a vehicle of unknown design, on which he bestowed the appelation of a four-wheeled phaeton, Nicholas proceeded on his journey next morning with greater ease than he had expected: the manager and himself occupying the front seat, and the Crummleses and Smike being packed together behind, in company with a wicker basket defended from wet by a stout oilskin, in which were the broadswords, pistols, pigtails, nautical costumes, and other professional necessaries of the aforesaid young gentleman."

In bed Miss Ormsby lay the book down and sipped some Johnny Walker. It was, alas, becoming more and more difficult to concentrate on Dickens. The length of his sentences sometimes defeated her; in the midst of all those clauses, one lost track of the subject. It was tiring and a great pity, for she had once so loved the man's prose. One year she adapted *A Christmas Carol* for the school concert. She herself had played Ebeneezer Scrooge, dressing up in an old frock coat and trousers. The pupils had laughed when she came on stage, though not, she liked to think, in an unkindly way. In any case, she hadn't cared a bean; she was having too much fun. Afterwards Mr. Pigeon congratulated her on what he termed "an enthusiastic performance."

She had poured over and loved all those English writers: Thackeray, Austen, Dickens, Hardy. She could see Tess walking with Angel down that dusty sunlit road. Or poor Elizabeth, left with the furmity woman in the tent after Henshaw's foolish wager. She could see the narrow streets of London where Oliver tried to escape from Bill Sykes. The scenery of England was as familiar in her mind as her own backyard, and these novels from another century had turned her into an Anglophile. England was a magical place that she dreamed of visiting. As a child she had opened her reader and there on the frontispiece was a picture of the Union Jack. During the war she had listened to the news from London read by Mathew Halton and Edward R. Murrow; she had heard the German bombs falling on the old city. She had imagined the trainloads of children leaving Euston station for the countryside. At school assembly she had sung with lusty voice "Land of Hope and Glory" and "Rule Britannia." She had dreamed of William and Dorothy Wordsworth walking at night above the rushing waters near Tintern Abbey.

> *Therefore let the moon*
> *Shine on thee in thy solitary walk;*
> *And let the misty, mountain winds be free*
> *To blow against thee:*

It was the little island that produced such giants as Shakespeare and Milton and Keats. Yet it seemed to take a lifetime to get there. To cross an ocean in an airplane seemed like such an enormous undertaking, and in fact she was past fifty before it was accomplished. She and Adelaide Bales finally made up their minds, and all that winter they planned the excursion, pouring over schedules and brochures, tremendously excited by the prospect. What she discovered when she got there was a London busier and dirtier than she could ever have imagined. The air was dense with diesel fumes and the streets were filled with young women in miniskirts and young men in flared trousers. That summer the music of the Beatle people was everywhere, and a kind of joyous vibrancy was in the air of England. Miss Ormsby was entranced. Behind all this soiled glitter she could see the London of old. In the courtyards and cramped streets near the river she could picture old Dr. Johnson walking about, his great brow furrowed as he worked out the design of his dictionary.

Adelaide, however, was sorely disappointed. She was a poor traveller, grumpy with constipation and flummoxed by the customs and currency of the land. Ever fearful of being cheated, she counted her money each night in the hotel room, laying out the large bank notes on the bed. They stayed at a hotel in Russell Square near the British Museum. Adelaide preferred the bus tours; her short powerful legs were inclined to swell after walking and she grumbled. Miss Ormsby, a seasoned walker, preferred the streets. Adelaide, so bold and preemptive at home, the terror of classroom and butcher shop, was timid among strangers. At night she sulked in the hotel room and after drinks and supper went to bed and snored mercilessly. Miss Ormsby sat by the window, kept awake by her companion's great snorts, but too excited really to mind, imagining as she looked down at the empty three o'clock streets, a Dickens or Hardy wandering restlessly while he tried to work out a plot complication.

One day, worn out from walking, they took refuge from the noise and diesel exhaust in a cinema off Tottenham Court Road. Adelaide confessed that she couldn't manage another step without resting. The poster advertised a film called *Persuasion*, and Miss Ormsby thought that a picture based on Jane Austen's novel would be invigorating for both of them. In the dark smoky theatre the two women stumbled over figures to get to their seats. The old black and white film looked shaky and of dubious quality. Was it foreign? wondered Miss Ormsby as she settled into her seat. Adelaide had sighed with relief as she sat down.

As both grew accustomed to the gloom, however, they became aware of something untoward, even sinister. Across the column of smoke from the lights of the projector, on the screen before them, lay what appeared to be a large white hill. But then the white hill moved and assumed the lineaments of a pair of buttocks. In time these

87

were seen to belong to a man who was engaged in an act of copulation with another man. Moreover, as the camera pulled back, a third man, naked except for leather gauntlets and boots, began to beat the copulating pair across the haunches with a hunting crop. This episode provoked a gasp from Adelaide at whom Miss Ormsby had cast a sideways glance. Behind the thick glasses was a look of amazed revulsion. Both women immediately arose and returned to the street.

It had been, of course, a terrible mistake, and Adelaide was loath to let Miss Ormsby forget it. An accomplished scold at the best of times, Adelaide now vented her frustration over the entire holiday: England and its people were impossible, and the film they had glimpsed was simply additional evidence of a society in moral decline. "Never in all my days," was how Adelaide began each account of *that afternoon*, as she referred to it. She sounded like some fiery Presbyterian pamphleteer. "Such persons should be locked up. They are defilers of decency. Flogging is too good for them. Why had Miss Ormsby not read the advertising material more carefully?"

In her bed at Sunset Manor Miss Ormsby sipped whiskey and smiled. In many ways it had been a shocking experience. Yet it *had been* an experience and an interesting one in its own way. Was it not Coleridge who said that we must embrace all experience in the quest for fulfillment? And when Miss Ormsby thought about *that afternoon*, as she had from time to time over the years, she concluded that it was all rather amusing. She had even tried to make her friend see this side of it. There was, maintained Miss Ormsby, a droll aspect to the experience if you chose to look at it from a certain angle. Two middle-aged spinsters from Canada find themselves by honest error in a pornographic movie house in London! But Adelaide would not be appeased and made Miss Ormsby promise never to tell a soul: "It would be a mortal embarrassment," she said. "You must never tell anyone, Kay." Miss Ormsby promised and of course kept her word.

Adelaide had cheered up, however, when they left London and went into the countryside. They took a coach tour to various literary landmarks. Miss Ormsby had wanted to rent a car, but Adelaide was afraid they would have an accident and return to Canada as cripples. And so they sat next to German and American widows, looking out the wide coach windows at stone cottages and fields of sheep. They ate buns and jam in tea shops and again climbed aboard the coach for the next village. They passed through Hardy's Dorset and Coleridge's Somerset; they visited Grasmere and Dove Cottage where the Wordsworths had lived. They saw the Brontë sisters' Yorkshire and were herded about Shakespeare's Stratford-on-Avon.

Adelaide was better-tempered on the coach. With her wide bottom wedged into the seat, she sipped prune juice and lectured her fellow passengers; she had done her homework and knew more about England than the tour guide. By the window Miss Ormsby sat adrift, thinking of Allan Webb. Once he told her that he would return to England and live in a cottage on the wild Devon coast where he had been born. He would write poetry in the mornings and in the afternoons, he would walk along the cliffs in the wind and the rain. After he told her that, the word Devon had a special place in her heart. On that first trip, however, she saw only a small part of the shire, for it wasn't on their tour. Adelaide gave everyone a lesson on Devon cream and how it was famous throughout the world. Poor talkative, opinionated Adelaide! Now with the others beneath the snow of Bayview Cemetery.

Miss Ormsby finished her whiskey and put *Nicholas Nickleby* on the little side table. She could hear the music from the gymnasium. Imagine having a dance in this place! She had never been much for dancing. When she was on monitor duty at the Friday night school dances, she had looked on with wry amusement at the young couples, clinging to each other with eyes closed as they shuffled about the gym in stockinged feet, listening to the quavering falsetto voice.

> *Earth angel, earth angel*
> *Will you be mine?*

When she was twenty or so, she had gone a few times to the Parkview Pavilion with Gladys Springer. But neither of them was ever asked to dance, and by ten o'clock they were having raisin pie and coffee at the Blue Parrot. This music, however, reminded her of the war and the Moore boys next door. For a couple of years the Moores rented the house next to them. The oldest boy, Tommy, joined the Army and later came back from England with a war bride, a pale pretty girl with strawberry blond hair who couldn't stand the Canadian winters and eventually returned home with her child.

On summer nights from her bedroom Miss Ormsby could see across the dark yard to the lighted house. Apart from Tommy, there were six or seven others in the family, and the boys, teenagers at the time, had their bedroom opposite Miss Ormsby's. They never pulled down the blind, and she could see the bare light bulb and the balsa wood model airplanes hanging by slender threads from the ceiling. She was thirty years old and felt vaguely ashamed to be kneeling by her bedroom window, looking across at the brown naked backs of the Moore boys as they listened to dance music on the radio. From the verandah came her father's voice as he talked to the Martinsons or Mr. Colby. She could smell the pipe smoke as it mingled with the scent of the yellow roses and the mock orange.

The Moores went to Mass every Sunday morning, the girls in their starched dresses and the boys in trousers and white shirts, their combed hair still wet from the bathtub.

Miss Ormsby's father used to shake his head at the peculiar rituals of Roman Catholics. On those summer Sunday mornings Miss Ormsby would sit at the Heintzman, attempting to remember the tunes her mother had tried to teach her. Bach for a Sunday morning! *Wachet auf, ruft uns die Stimme.* As she drifted into sleep, Miss Ormsby remembered attempting it.

SEVEN

Mrs. Lucas was certain that the snow would provide Ward and Irma with an excuse for not visiting. They would phone later and tell her that the streets were too icy. They were always looking for an excuse not to visit. "They won't be here today, you mark my words," said Mrs. Lucas to no one in particular. It was Sunday afternoon and she was sitting by the windows in the Sun Room, watching the wind blow the snow across the parking lot. She had spoken these words aloud, a habit she had recently acquired. Now and then, for no reason that she or anyone else could discover, she would send a few sentences into thin air. But if anyone, including the nursing staff at Sunset Manor, took any notice, they didn't let on. Odd behaviour, as long as it didn't become violent, was by and large tolerated with good-humoured patience by the institution.

Mrs. Lucas felt like going over to Mrs. Huddle and Mrs. Somers and telling them about the snow. They were looking at the television where skindivers were swimming along the floor of a tropical sea. There were any number of strange-looking creatures and fishes in this watery world, and the two old ladies were gazing intently at the screen. Mrs. Lucas decided that neither of them would care about the snow that was now swirling in gusts beyond the windows. Mrs. Huddle received no visitors, and though Mrs. Somers had sons and daughters, she rarely saw any of them. Nor did their absence appear to bother her in the least. Mrs. Somers was possessed of such an even temperament that nothing appeared to affect her. Either that, or she had abandoned any interest in the outside world. Mrs. Lucas could not be sure; she knew only that Mrs. Somers's nature often irritated her to the point where she would have enjoyed giving the woman the shaking of her life.

There were cars with their lights on turning into the parking lot. Their clogged windshield wipers could barely clear the snow from the windows. It had stormed all weekend, and watching the cars, Mrs. Lucas decided that if some could take the trouble to drive through the snow, then so could Ward and Irma. Thinking about this, Mrs. Lucas began to compose a little speech which she planned to deliver at the first opportunity. This address was intended for her son, and had to do with the indisputable fact that his mother would not be around forever, and that he might well regret not having visited her on a snowy Sunday in December. Inventing this little speech and imagining the look on Ward's face was immensely satisfying.

Just then, however, she looked up and saw her son in the hallway. He was carrying his coat and overshoes. His scarf was still around his neck. Mrs. Lucas watched him as he hung up his coat on a rack of hangers provided for guests. He placed his overshoes beneath the coat and advanced across the Sun Room towards her. Ward had become stout in middle age; in his fifties he had grown dewlaps, and Mrs. Lucas thought her son looked clumsy and old. She preferred to remember him as a little boy setting off for his first day of school in stiff new clothes. When he left for school there was always the smell of petunias in the air, and whenever she thought of those flowers, Mrs. Lucas remembered her son and Septembers long past. He had been such a neat and tidy little boy.

He was so unlike Joan, who couldn't stay out of the dirt. You couldn't keep a clean pair of underpants on that girl. She was always squatting on the sidewalk to pet a cat or look at an anthill or some similar foolishness. When she stood up, of course, her underpants were filthy. Those underpants were like a reproach. Mrs. Lucas had long been convinced that her daughter had done such things on purpose. She had always been a spiteful child. Now Ward was different; he never gave her a speck of trouble in that regard. Always turned his pockets inside out before putting his trousers in the clothes hamper on Saturday nights before his bath. Always wore his rubbers on rainy days and took his shoes off at the door. And now here he was walking towards her, a plump elderly man. In a way, thought Mrs. Lucas, it was remarkable. At the same time, of course, it wasn't, for everyone gets old. That was a fact of life.

Ward looked aggrieved and unhappy, but then he nearly always did nowadays. He nodded to her. "So how are you today, Mother?" he asked. "Irma couldn't make it, I'm afraid. Deborah has come down with a bad cold. She went out last night half-dressed. We told her to put on clothes for the weather, but she wouldn't pay any attention. Now she's in bed with a temperature and she'll probably stay there for the holidays. These damn kids don't listen to a word you tell them."

Mrs. Lucas nodded impatiently, waiting for her son to finish. She had a great deal on her mind and was eager to get under way. They sat in the orange chairs by the windows. There was to be no cake or cookies today it seemed. Well, they had a sick child on their hands and she supposed that could account for the oversight.

Ward avoided her eye. He hated visiting this place. Mrs. Lucas could sense that by the grim cast of his features and by the manner in which he jiggled his right knee and looked uneasy. He never stayed long. You worked your fingers to the bone. You raised children. You made any God's number of sacrifices for them. You buried the man you lived with for forty-five years and sold the house you'd slaved in for most of your life. And at the end of it all, nobody could spend half an hour a week with you!

Mrs. Lucas watched her son, who was looking out at the parking lot and the turbulent afternoon. She leaned forward suddenly and said, "Ward, you won't believe what's happened!"

Her son opened his mouth as if to speak, but seemed to think better of it, for instead he frowned at her. "As if," said Mrs. Lucas, "Lorne Truscott wasn't enough of a trial, there's now a woman on the other side of me who, I'm convinced of it, is not right in the head. She wears an orange wig and she smokes cigarettes by the handful. She keeps me awake half the night chanting."

Ward Lucas narrowed his eyes. "Chanting, Mother?"

"I've spoken to Mrs. Rawlings about it, but that woman isn't interested in the welfare of those under her care." Mrs. Lucas sat back and paused for breath. There was a stitch in her side and she had to sit back to relieve the pressure. "You might just as well talk to this chair as say a word to her. She pays no attention whatsoever to the concerns of the residents."

"But you're always going to her, Mother," said Ward Lucas. "Did it ever occur to you that perhaps Mrs. Rawlings gets tired of always hearing your complaints?"

Mrs. Lucas looked affronted. "Well goodness knows it's her job, Ward, to listen to the complaints of the residents." The soundness of this observation struck her as worthy enough to bear repetition. "That's surely what the woman is paid to do. Listen to the complaints of those who pay her wages. I put out good money for my room. I don't see why

I should have to live next to people who bang on my walls in the middle of the night."

"Is this woman banging on your walls, Mother?" asked Ward Lucas.

Mrs. Lucas shook her head, exasperated by her son's obtuseness.

"No, no, no, I'm talking about Lorne Truscott. That man will be the death of me, Ward," she added, wagging a forefinger at her son who appeared to sag a little in his chair. He said, "I've been hearing about Lorne Truscott for two years now. Look Mother, Lorne's something of a character. I've told you that time and time again. Everybody in town knows that. He's just trying to get under your skin. If you ignored him, he wouldn't even bother you probably."

"I cannot," said Mrs. Lucas firmly, "ignore someone who bangs on my walls in the middle of the night and who has chairs that are advertised on the television delivered to my door. Along with Chinese dinners and pizza pies at eleven o'clock at night. I've had rock and roll records and vegetable cutters come through the mail to me."

Mrs. Lucas stopped as if suddenly aware that she was babbling, and that she herself could be adjudged incoherent and unstable. Trying to put a more reasonable face on these matters she said, "The woman with the orange hair smokes like a fiend, and one night she'll burn the place down, you mark my words. There ought to be regulations against smoking in a building like this, and I've a good mind to phone the fire department and make inquiries. She's up there half the night smoking and chanting."

Ward Lucas began to entertain the uncomfortable notion that his mother was at last losing her grip on reality. For years his wife had prophesied just such an eventuality. "What is she chanting, Mother?" asked Ward Lucas. "It seems hard to believe."

"I haven't the faintest idea what she's chanting," said

Mrs. Lucas. "I just hear this low droning sound. My feeling is that she can't be right in the head. She's a maiden lady after all, and when they get old, they sometimes get strange in their ways. They haven't lived normal lives, if you know what I mean." Ward Lucas had no idea what his mother was talking about, and his puzzled expression bore witness to this.

"Her name's Ormsby," continued Mrs. Lucas. "She taught up at the high school for years. We got another teacher in here too. Arthur Wilkie is on the third floor. Everybody in town knows about that old goat."

"I remember Miss Ormsby," said Ward Lucas. "She taught me in Grade Twelve. A thin, tall, red-headed woman. She always smelled of cheap perfume or toilet water. There were those who said that she wasn't too particular about herself. She lived with her father in that big brick house over on Park Street."

Ward Lucas was again looking out at the storm. He had not worn a hat and his hair was still damp from the snow. Staring at him, Mrs. Lucas felt overcome by tenderness and pity for herself and for all creatures under the sun. When you thought about it, life was mostly burdensome, and then you grew old and weak and vulnerable; you became easy prey for the Truscotts and the Rawlings of this world. Mrs. Lucas could no longer hold back the tears that were now leaking from her eyes. And after all, it did feel good to cry. Life was unfair, and she could give them chapter and verse on it too.

Mrs. Lucas wept quietly as she looked at the falling snow. "I don't see why I can't have that back bedroom, Ward," she said softly. "I'd be on my own. I can look after myself. I could even help with the meals."

Ward Lucas looked around the Sun Room as though fearful of being heard, although in fact no one was paying them any mind. "You know how impossible that is,

Mother," he said. "We've been through all this before, so why bring it up?"

His mother offered only her tearful profile, and Ward Lucas leaned forward to hand her a tissue. His grave whispers were charged with irritation.

"We're doing the best we can, Mother. You have no idea what it's like these days. The kids! They get on Irma's nerves. And our house is not as big as it looks. It's not easy."

Mrs. Lucas said nothing to this. The truth was that she detested the whine in her son's voice.

"You bring this up every time I come here," said Ward Lucas. "It isn't fair. We're doing the best we can."

"I'm sure you are, Ward," said Mrs. Lucas, removing her glasses and dabbing at her eyes with a tissue. Without the glasses, her eyes looked astonishingly large and naked. "I'm sure you are," repeated Mrs. Lucas, returning the glasses to her face.

Ward Lucas leaned back and looked around the Sun Room, which was now half-filled with visitors; most of them were men and women his age. They sat on the sofas and orange chairs talking to the old folks. Others stared at the television.

"I see they've put up a nice tree in the dining room," said Ward Lucas. He was fighting to overcome a bleakness of spirit that threatened to leave his Sunday in ruins. "The big day will soon be here," he said. "Now what would you like for Christmas, Mother? Irma made me promise to ask."

Mrs. Lucas was ready for this. "Oh don't go to any trouble for me," she said.

"It's no trouble Mother."

"I might not even be around for Christmas," said Mrs. Lucas. "I have these terrible pains."

Ward Lucas stared at his mother's profile with dull dislike in his eyes. He had heard all this before many times, and it was nothing less than a trial and a tribulation to sit here every Sunday and go over it again and again.

"Have you seen the doctor, Mother?" he asked.

"Doctors aren't interested in the elderly," said Mrs. Lucas. "They don't care whether we live or die."

"I'm sure that's not true," said Ward Lucas, who had now lost any interest whatsoever in the conversation. He was anxious to be on his way, and accordingly stood up. "I'd better go now, Mother," he said. "That snow is not letting up. I'll have to get the blower out into the driveway."

"Yes . . . well," said Mrs. Lucas vaguely. Ward Lucas leaned over and kissed his mother's damp cheek. "I'll be around Christmas eve morning to pick you up, Mother. Now you take care, ok?"

Mrs. Lucas nodded, but said not a word of farewell. Let him go back to his four-bedroom house and his snowblower and all the rest of it. He didn't have to live next door to Lorne Truscott and a woman with an orange wig who chanted in the night. He didn't have to deal with Rawlings or eat food that gave you gas cramps so bad you could burst. This affliction now forced her to lift a buttock, the better to ease the passage of a little wind. A mercy when that happened!

Mrs. Lucas turned from the window to look across the Sun Room. Lorne Truscott was now standing next to Mrs. Huddle and Mrs. Somers, who were still seated in front of the television. Truscott had one hand in his trouser pocket and was digging at himself. It was disgusting, and with visitors around too. That morning Mrs. Lucas had listened to Pastor Bob enumerate the various punishments that lay ahead for sinners condemned to eternal damnation. "The walls of Hell are mighty thick," said Pastor Bob, "and the fire and smoke something awful. Think of that movie *The Towering Inferno*," he said. "The one with Paul Newman and Steve McQueen. Think of the fiery scenes in that movie and then multiply them *a hundred million times*. Then you might get some idea of the heat within the walls of Hell. Sinners will pray for a glass of cold water. But there'll be none. *There is no cold water in Hell*," said Pastor Bob. "Just eternal damnation and heat you wouldn't believe."

Mrs. Lucas thought that all of it was too good for the likes of Lorne Truscott.

"Did I ever tell you ladies," said Lorne Truscott, sinking into a chair beside Mrs. Huddle and Mrs. Somers, "that I once played in an exhibition game against the Montreal Maroons? Now mind you, I'm not talking about the Montreal Canadiens. They're a different bunch altogether, Frenchmen mostly. I'm talking now about the Maroons. They haven't been around since the late thirties, but I played in an exhibition game against them in the fall of 1934. We played them in the Kingston Arena, a senior all-star team. Snuffy Coles sent me down because he thought I might catch someone's eye. Christ Almighty, I never even got a shot on net! The Maroons beat the living shit out of us. I think the final score was twelve to two. Hooley Smith must have had five or six goals himself. Jesus Christ, you talk about a crazy man on skates! That son of a bitch could fly. And sneaky with the stick too. Mean as a polecat with a feather up his ass. He'd give you that stick in the gizzard if you got in his way."

Lorne stretched out his legs and laced his fingers across his belly. "They had a team that year, believe you me. They had Ward and Trottier. Baldy Northcott. Lionel Conacher. They won the Cup the next spring. They beat Smythe's Leafs three straight games. I won twenty-five dollars at the Foundry in that series. Everybody was a goddamn Toronto fan. Do you remember, Mrs. H.? Saturday nights around the old Marconi?" Lorne now cupped his hands to his mouth and imitated a radio announcer of bygone days. "Hello Canada and hockey fans from coast to coast," Lorne shouted. "It's the second period and Montreal is leading the Leafs one to nothing on a goal by Northcott from Ward and Trottier."

Some of the visitors looked askance at these shenanigans, but Mrs. Huddle and Mrs. Somers ignored the performance. They were used to Lorne Truscott's antics and knew how to deal with them. Lorne was like a barking dog; if you ignored him, he eventually went away. Nurse Fox, however, came over and told Lorne that if he didn't behave himself, he would have to leave the Sun Room. The ladies were now watching a program on Japan. The screen offered the view of a street in downtown Tokyo. Through what looked like shimmering heat, a million Japanese pedestrians were marching towards the TV audience. What did it all mean?

Lorne guessed that the weather had kept his granddaughter and the kids from coming, though they had missed last Sunday and the Sunday before that too. He looked at a scene in a Japanese steel mill. Enormous showers of sparks surrounded little men in hard hats as they withdrew bright bars of steel from forges. Those fuckers were running the world now, thought Lorne. Take Moreton itself! Where would the town be without the colour TV factory and the seat belt place. They were both owned by the Japs. In the old days you had the Shipyard and the Flour Mill. There was the Foundry and the grain elevators and Begg's Lumberyard. All owned by Canadians. Or at least by white men. It was a son of a bitch the way the world had changed in the last forty years.

Watching the Japanese steelworkers reminded Lorne of the day in the Foundry when a keg of nails fell on his foot and broke three toes. He was off work for the rest of that winter and couldn't play hockey. He helped Snuffy with the coaching and there was always time for tomfoolery. Like the night he put the mouse in Ernie Dillion's skate. Ernie nearly shit a brick when he stuck his foot in that skate. Somebody pissed in the water bottle that year, but it wasn't him. He had a scrap with Bert Rennie over that. He'd been in lots of fights in the old Arena, some on the ice and some in the stands when Billy was playing. There was the night Billy was playing midget and he scored four goals against Collingwood. And Lorne was sitting right in the middle of that Collingwood gang and giving it to them. Now that was a night!

Lorne Truscott tried not to think about his oldest son and the night the policeman came to the door to tell him about the accident. "I told him to buy a car and not a goddamn motorcycle," Lorne told the policeman, though why he said that was a mystery. It was all a goddamn mystery when it came right down to it. Lorne stirred in his chair and looked at the screen where people in kimonos were sitting on the floor of a little room drinking tea from cups without handles. What a bunch of goddamn foolishness! Lorne got to his feet, and leaning over Mrs. Huddle, crooned a few bars of "Ricochet Romance." Then he left the Sun Room, though not before he turned his Yankee cap around and contorted his features into the comical grimace that had entertained fans between innings at the ball diamond thirty years ago.

On Sunday afternoons Mr. Wilkie preferred his room and his puzzle books. At such times Sunset Manor was astir with women who still fancied themselves prospective brides. They wore scent and earrings and simpered like schoolgirls. Preposterous as it might seem, Kay Ormsby was now amongst them, turned out very likely in finery that had been chosen especially to entice the unwary. Mr. Wilkie did not care to be in the Sun Room to witness such nonsense. Instead he had removed his hearing appliance and now sat by the window overlooking Transit Road and the shopping centre. On such occasions he sometimes liked to think about his dead wife and particularly of the years before she was consigned to a wheelchair.

He saw her as a young blonde woman whom he met one summer while working in an office on King Street in Toronto. Ada's uncle was a partner in the firm, and like Mr. Wilkie, she was working there for the summer. She told him that it helped to pass the time. Ada was a bored languid young woman, and in a physical sense, he was not attracted to her. He preferred women with more flesh on their bones. There were, however, points in Ada's favour. For one thing she was due to inherit a great deal of money, and for another she was tall. Mr. Wilkie believed that a tall man should have a tall partner in life; to do otherwise would render an injustice to the laws of proportion. There was also an air of regal calm about Ada that he found alluring. She was never in a hurry, nor did she ever display anxiety over trivial misfortunes like missed taxis or late appointments. Her entire manner suggested that the world could wait for her and mostly it did.

Ada wore her hair bobbed that summer and her slender neck was lovely. With her long legs and fine neck, she was like a kind of bird. In fact, when she stepped delicately around the office, dipping her cropped head into filing cabinets, she reminded Mr. Wilkie of some large wading bird, a crane perhaps or a heron. There was nothing for it but to court this aristocratic creature and meet her family. And this he did on a summer evening so enriched by gaiety and promise that its very moments were still vivid in his memory.

Ada's mother, a tall gray-haired woman in a mauve dress, received him in the drawing room of the house in Rosedale. The windows were open to admit the fragrant evening air; through the leafy trees beyond these windows, pale light entered and wavered across the tables and chairs and carpet. There were flowers in vases, and from another part of the house came laughter and the voice of Rudy Vallee singing on a gramophone record. To Mr. Wilkie's delight, the house in Rosedale was filled with women. Ada's father was dead, but there were several sisters and aunts and cousins and maids. Mr. Wilkie, who had never felt at home among the male rough and tumble of locker rooms or smokers, was quite at ease in this agreeable world of females. He watched proudly as Ada broke a piece of coffee cake with her long white fingers. Tea was served by a husky dark girl who was probably of Italian origin. As she lay the refreshments before them, Mr. Wilkie was inspired by the sight of her hands and the dark hair that curled about her ears. Nevertheless he proposed marriage to Ada later that evening.

How could anyone have forecast on that fragrant summer evening that within two years there would be so much misfortune within the family? Ada's mother would be dead and the family fortune lost in the crash of '29. Beyond that lay Ada's polio and the wheelchair and his return to a lifetime of fractions and decimal points at Moreton District High School. Turning from the window, Mr. Wilkie picked up his puzzle book and with his fountain pen began to scratch furiously at figures. The assignment was to compute the time required for three travellers, journeying from afar and by various modes of transportation, to reach the city of London. The matter was complicated, of course, by the differing velocities of each vehicle and by the change in time zones.

Miss Ormsby had been listening to Brahms and her heart was quite full. At the knock on the door she blinked her damp, shining eyes and crossed the room. Mrs. Rawlings smiled in at her. She was wearing a canary yellow pants suit. "I hope, Miss Ormsby, that this is not an inopportune time," said Mrs. Rawlings, glancing around the room and sniffing the air which smelled of cigarette smoke and Miss Ormsby's own peculiar body salts. Books and records spilled from boxes and the ashtray was full. Miss Ormsby, in an old green dress, was barefoot, her hair uncombed. "You must forgive me, Mrs. Rawlings," she said, "but I'm scarcely presentable yet. I have been listening to Brahms. The Andante movement of his C Minor piano quartet. Number three. It's very, very beautiful and never fails to move me."

Miss Ormsby walked to the window and stood looking out at the snow. "Where would we be without beauty, Mrs. Rawlings?" she asked. "Even the falling snow on a Sunday afternoon is a kind of poetry." She continued to stare out of the window. "As I listened to Brahms, I thought of Lear's final speech. Do you know it, Mrs. Rawlings?" At the window in the pale winter light Miss Ormsby opened both hands and addressed a deranged world.

> *And my poor fool is hanged! No, no, no life!*
> *Why should a dog, a horse, a rat have life,*
> *And thou no breath at all? Thou'll come no more,*
> *Never, never, never, never, never!*

Miss Ormsby smiled gravely at Mrs. Rawlings. "Very beautiful, Mrs. Rawlings. Very moving. Such words can only elevate us. Don't you agree?"

Was the woman drunk at this hour of the day, wondered Mrs. Rawlings? She didn't smell of drink or of that horrible sen sen flavour used often by Lorne Truscott. The whiskey bottle on the table still looked half-full, but perhaps there were others hidden away. Miss Ormsby seemed lost in thought, and after a moment Mrs. Rawlings said, "I myself enjoy classical music. As a matter of fact, it's the very subject that brings me to your room. I'm afraid, Miss Ormsby, that there have been complaints."

Miss Ormsby appeared to have recovered her wits, for

she turned to look steadily at Mrs. Rawlings. "I'm glad to hear you say that you enjoy good music, Mrs. Rawlings. I'm sure you're not alone. There must be dozens of others in this place who want some musical nourishment. As I said the other morning, I can really see no reason at all why we should have to listen to such poor stuff in the halls. It's like the dentist's office or the supermarket. Could mere silence not prevail, Mrs. Rawlings? Could we not eat our breakfast without 'Raindrops Keep Fallin' on My Head'? Or failing silence, could we not have a little Bach or Handel in the mornings? Some Vivaldi? Something to awaken and refesh the heart?"

Mrs. Rawlings smiled knowingly. "I'm afraid I must disagree with you there, Miss Ormsby. Sunset Manor subscribes to the most popular FM station in the area. Surveys show that it's by far the favourite with the over fifty-five set. A day seldom goes by when a resident doesn't tell me how much he or she enjoys the lovely music."

"Is that so?" said Miss Ormsby, turning again to the window. "I find that rather disheartening. I wonder if it's true."

"May I," said Mrs. Rawlings, "just reiterate what I said to you the other day, Miss Ormsby? You are very new to the facility and it strikes me that you must get used to sharing space with others. I can appreciate how difficult that must be for someone who has lived alone for so many years."

Was Miss Ormsby listening? Again she seemed buried in thought. She had absently reached for a cigarette and lit it. She would miss her walk today; it was simply too blustery. There was ice under that snow and she could fall. At her age that could mean months of recovery. Osteoporosis was doubtless hollowing out her bones at that very moment. And where after all could one walk in this godforsaken place? The shopping plaza? The suburban streets offered neither sidewalk nor tree. Miss Ormsby

106

warned herself not to despair; she must not allow herself to be defeated. She would have to get used to these surroundings. She had no choice in the matter. And, after all, tomorrow was another day! She had a ten o'clock appointment at Beaux Arts; her hair really was a fright. She would take the bus downtown and visit the library. And the liquor store for fresh supplies. There were things to do, and she would not allow herself to become discouraged. But what was this tiresome woman going on about? Complaints? Complaints about what and by whom?

"Mrs. Lucas is rather frail," said Mrs. Rawlings.

"Mrs. Lucas?" said Miss Ormsby. "Is that the woman next door? She looks as strong as an ox to me."

"I am," said Mrs. Rawlings, "referring to the state of her nerves, Miss Ormsby. She is not a well woman. And now she has trouble sleeping because of your music and other sounds in the night."

"Other sounds, Mrs. Rawlings?" asked Miss Ormsby stubbing out her cigarette.

"Yes," said Mrs. Rawlings. "Mrs. Lucas says she hears chanting sounds in the night."

"Chanting sounds!" said Miss Ormsby. "What on earth can she be referring to, unless . . ." Miss Ormsby smiled. "Perhaps she is referring to the poetry. Sometimes I read poetry aloud, Mrs. Rawlings. That must be it."

Chanting! She had always thought that she read poetry rather well, yet next door was someone who heard Shakespeare and Wordsworth only as random noise. On the other hand, thought Miss Ormsby, perhaps I do get carried off on the wings of poesy at times.

"I shall try *to chant* more quietly, Mrs. Rawlings," she said, "and I shall turn down my music."

Mrs. Rawlings smiled triumphantly. "Miss Ormsby, I so appreciate your cooperation." Glancing at the wall behind her she lowered her voice. "Mrs. Lucas is a dear lady, but I fear she doesn't share our passion for the arts."

107

"I understand," said Miss Ormsby.

"Excellent. I'm so glad we had this little talk. I have always believed, and I am now speaking after twenty-five years in the administration of care for seniors, that communication is the key to successful relationships. Keep lines of communication open and everyone benefits." Mrs. Rawlings's gimlet eye fell upon the little tire ashtray. "You will be careful about the cigarettes won't you, Miss Ormsby?"

"I shall endeavour not to burn down the facility, Mrs. Rawlings."

"Absolutely splendid," said Mrs. Rawlings. "What more can I say?"

EIGHT

The sun on the snow was too much for Mrs. Lucas, and sitting by the windows in the Sun Room, she had closed her eyes against the glaring light. A man astride a machine was clearing away the snow; he was pushing it into great piles in the corners of the parking lot. The monotonous drone of his contraption and the morning sunlight streaming through the windows had made Mrs. Lucas drowsy, and finally she slept, snoring a little in her chair.

When she awakened, Clark Gable was standing over her. He was smiling and softly calling her name. With his carefully combed black hair and moustache, he was indeed handsome to behold. He offered his hand and Mrs. Lucas shook it. "Mrs. Lucas?" said the young man. "Hi! My name's Gary Polk. May I sit down?"

Mrs. Lucas nodded and the young man sat in the chair opposite her. He wasn't of course Clark Gable at all; the famous actor had passed away many years ago. Yet this Gary Polk did resemble him in many ways. Upon awakening abruptly, a person could certainly be forgiven for mistaking this young man for the old cinema star. "I must have nodded off," said Mrs. Lucas, who felt mildly ashamed of herself. Sleeping in the middle of the morning! What must this young man think of her?

"That's easy enough to do," said Gary Polk. For a moment he shielded his eyes with a hand. "That sun on the snow is really bright, isn't it?" he said, returning the hand to his lap and grinning boyishly.

Looking around the empty Sun Room Mrs. Lucas wished that Mrs. Huddle and Mrs. Somers could see her talking to this handsome young man. "When I was a little girl," said Mrs. Lucas, "I would make angels in the snow on a morning like this. My mother would dress me in a coat and leggings and scarf and mittens, and I would go out and flop in the snow and make angels. You lay on your back and spread your arms and legs . . ." It didn't sound right the way she'd put that; in fact, it sounded downright indecent, and anyway, why for goodness sakes was she going on about her childhood to a perfect stranger? As if to atone for this lapse in taste, Mrs. Lucas added, "I wasn't always old you know."

There was a hint of surliness in her voice, but the young man only said, "You're not old, Mrs. Lucas. Whoever told you that?"

"I'll be seventy-nine next March twelfth," said Mrs. Lucas. Gary Polk wagged his sleek head in disbelief. "You gotta be kidding," he said. "Do you know something Mrs. Lucas?" he added.

"What's that?" asked Mrs. Lucas.

"I deal with seniors every day," said Gary Polk. "Believe you me, I see hundreds of folks like you every week of my life. If you'll forgive me for boasting a little, *I know seniors*. And in my considered opinion, I would not put you past seventy. Not a day, believe me."

This observation provoked a dry bark of laughter in Mrs. Lucas. "You must be an Irishman," she said, "with that kind of blarney." Behind the rimless glasses, however, her eyes had narrowed in suspicion at that very possibility; all her life Mrs. Lucas had mistrusted the Irish, believing that their way with words masked a multitude of sins beginning with deceit and ending with indolence. She was, however, enjoying the young man's banter. He had now settled a briefcase upon his lap and was withdrawing various papers from it. Evidently he was peddling something; they were supposed to stop the salesmen at the front door, but this one had obviously slipped through the net.

Mrs. Lucas frowned. They had been having such a nice conversation, and now he would try to sell her something that she didn't need. Well, no fear of that; she would give him his marching orders in due course. Salesmen seldom got the better of her. Now with George it was different. He had no more sales resistance than a pup; he couldn't say no to anyone. Still, Mr. Polk was a nice young man, and it was a pleasant change to talk to someone from a younger generation. Goodness knows her grandchildren seldom bothered to visit her; they always had something else to do it seemed. Mrs. Lucas decided that if Gary Polk was selling Bibles, she would take one in the modestly priced range. A spare Bible around the place was surely no extravagance.

Gary Polk again offered his disarming smile. "I understand, Mrs. Lucas, that your husband passed away some time ago."

"He did," said Mrs. Lucas. "It will be ten years in January." Gary Polk stared at the carpeted Sun Room floor and looked thoughtful.

"I see," he said. "May I ask what arrangements were made?"

"Arrangements?" asked Mrs. Lucas. "How do you mean?"

The young man turned his genial gaze upon Mrs. Lucas. "May I ask if there was internment or cremation?"

"He's lying up in Bayview Cemetery. Why?" asked Mrs. Lucas who detested the subject of death.

"Memorial Gardens," said Gary Polk, "provides a new concept in preplanned departure servicing. We also offer an attractive package of bereavement benefits personally designed to fit each individual's needs. These include perpetual care of the departed one's resting place, and anniversary reminders for those who remain behind." The young man was now displaying a brochure that appeared to advertise headstones and memorial tablets. At the sight of these items Mrs. Lucas cried, "Why are you showing me these things?"

Gary Polk managed to look pleasantly puzzled. "Did you not call our office, Mrs. Lucas? Did you not ask to see a service representative?"

"I did no such thing," said Mrs. Lucas, who now felt a tightness in her chest. It was as though a score of iron hoops had encircled her and were now pressing the life from her lungs. This was Truscott's doing. That was plain as eggs. He had phoned these people and he would be responsible for the heart attack that she now felt she was having, though it could be just another gas pain, for her bowels hadn't moved in three days. Throughout this ordeal she had been leaning forward, and so now she eased herself back in the chair. The thickness around her heart vanished and she could breathe again. The sunlight glinted off her glasses. "You have made a mistake, young man," she said. "I have no interest whatsoever in your wares. Please leave at once."

Gary Polk, however, was no stranger to rejection, and was already gathering together his literature and returning it to his briefcase. "I am sorry, Mrs. Lucas," he said. His generous mouth and wide Clark Gable moustache seemed to droop, suggesting remorse, though this facial expression could have been and very likely was contrived. "You must understand," he said, "that Memorial Gardens was notified of your interest."

"So it would seem," said Mrs. Lucas, her face set sternly against the foolishness of this world. "However," she added, "I made no such inquiries."

Gary Polk arose, and on behalf of his employer and

himself, offered apologies for the misunderstanding. "You have," he said, "been the victim of a cruel hoax. I can only say that, personally speaking, it is not my idea of a joke."

There was nothing to say to that, and in her chair Mrs. Lucas nodded and watched the young man depart. At that very moment, however, a desperate plan had begun to take shape in her mind. She could see only its outline, but the details would doubtless come later. There had to be a way in which she could put something—weedkiller or rat poison—in his food. The mere idea of it thrilled her, as had nothing in recent memory.

The residents of Sunset Manor were having a party to decorate the Christmas tree. The maintenance people had put up an enormous fir tree in a corner of the dining room, and under the supervision of Mr. Jaffey and Mrs. Teagarden, a number of people were attaching to it coloured balls and candy cane and tinsel. The lights were already in place. The Sunset Choristers had arranged themselves into a group near the steam tables and were singing Christmas songs.

If he could find the mistletoe, Lorne Truscott threatened to kiss all the ladies, including the nurses and Mrs. Fenerty, who had been wheeled in to observe the proceedings. The old woman sat like a great spotted stone in the midst of the revelry, and was fussed over by one and all. Soon, however, she fell asleep in her chair. Instead of serving the usual hot dinner, the kitchen staff had provided plates of sandwiches and cake. There was also tea and fruit punch. None of this, however, sat well with Mr. Wilkie, who had arrived expecting to find the normal Monday fare of meatloaf with creamed potatoes and side vegetable followed by rice or tapioca pudding.

Mr. Wilkie stood by the dining hall entrance, a tall slightly stooped figure in gray trousers and jacket with a plaid weskit beneath. His long face was severe with disapproval. Sandwiches and cake was not his idea of adequate nutrition, and he had a good mind to speak to the administrator about it. Elderly citizens needed a proper diet to maintain themselves. How in Heaven's name could one be expected to last until supper on a few sandwiches and little cakes? It was an outrage to pay good money and not receive value. He wondered whether a letter to the local Board of Health might not be in order. It was often beneficial to remind people of promises made but not kept. Nor could he go out to the shopping plaza and eat a meal at The Chicken House today! The thermometer outside his window had registered fourteen degrees Fahrenheit at last reading. With his angina, it was no time to be outdoors. On such a day he could easily topple into a snowbank and perish. It wasn't fair, and the injustice of it set Mr. Wilkie's features to work; his face assumed an odd twisted look. He appeared indeed to be giving the very devil to some invisible enemy.

Across the dining hall Lorne Truscott noticed Mr. Wilkie's peculiar grimaces, and turning his baseball cap around, pulled some faces of his own in return. Mrs. Lucas was in his field of vision, and he hoped thereby to unsettle her as well. Lorne had seen the young man leave, and was now looking for signs of confusion and distress in Mrs. Lucas's demeanor. Instead he found her looking sly and oddly pleased with herself.

It was during such events as the Christmas tree party that Mrs. Rawlings liked to run a few spot checks on the residents' quarters. At such times she could nip in and out of the empty rooms and with no one any the wiser. Mrs. Rawlings liked to think that by so doing, she was keeping on top of things at Sunset Manor. She was no longer astonished at the secrets uncovered by these visits. At one time, perhaps, the gin bottles, the illicit novels, the vibrators, might have been cause for wonderment. But no longer. After a quarter of a century, Mrs. Rawlings had seen it all.

Laden with parcels, Miss Ormsby ignored the van driver who had stopped to shout something at her. The device in her ears prevented her from understanding a word the young man was saying, and judging by the expression on his face, that was probably just as well. Miss Ormsby had got off the bus at the shopping plaza and had, it seems, crossed against the light on Transit Road. But that was scarcely a reason for looking as *insane* as the young driver had. Miss Ormsby, however, refused to allow this incident to ruin an otherwise excellent day. She soon put it out of mind as she made her way carefully towards the entrance of Sunset Manor.

It was a bright cold afternoon, but Miss Ormsby was dressed for the weather. She knew a thing or two about taking care of herself in Ontario winters. Beneath the faded cloth coat were several sweaters. Her old fur-topped boots remained sturdy and reliable. There were two thicknesses of mittens on her hands. The green tam was pulled over her ears concealing the yellow Walkman that now flooded her brain with the light of a summer day. Von Karajan was conducting the Berlin Philharmonic in Beethoven's Sixth, and its pastoral calm was a feast for the soul. In her mind's eye Miss Ormsby saw a meadow of white and yellow flowers. Under a leafy tree rested a herd of black and white cattle. Nearby a clear stream travelled over pale stones. All of this may have accounted for the near mishap at the traffic lights.

The earphones transporting this enchantment from the little tape machine fastened to one of her sweaters was a kind of miracle. Or so it seemed to Miss Ormsby, who saw at once the solution to listening to music without disturbing her neighbour. It was true that she would now have to convert her record library to tape and that would cost money. But what of it? And anyway, many of her phonograph records were old and scratched; the machine itself was almost past use. It was surely time for a change; it was time "to get with it" as you heard people saying nowadays.

All of this Miss Ormsby found exhilarating. The day itself had been a triumph. Even the bus ride downtown had been enriched by the sight of the evergreens at the entrance to the park. Their dark branches were heavy with snow and on one of them perched a whiskey jack, a blue flame against the white and green. A small moment, but not to be missed! Then also the practical business of living had been attended to: Miss Ormsby had visited the hairdresser and various other establishments. In the parcels clasped against her chest was a bottle of Johnny Walker, a carton of Rothmans, and several library books and tapes. It was the Walkman, however, that had made Miss Ormsby's day. Its neatness and simplicity had quite overwhelmed her.

She normally bought very little in the way of consumer items. It wasn't parsimony that kept her from counter and showroom; it was more a lack of interest in the goods of this world. Over the years she had made do with whatever her parents had put into the house on Park Street. When things needed replacing, she saw to it and did not begrudge the expense. When Madden Fuels stopped selling coal, she arranged to have the furnace converted to oil and oversaw the installation of the brick-coloured storage tank in the fruit cellar. When the round-shouldered and yellowing refrigerator finally stopped one day, she immediately bought a new one, taking the first model shown to her by the salesman. "That one will do," said Miss Ormsby. And why not? Wasn't one refrigerator much the same as another? Weren't there other things to do in life beside choosing refrigerators?

Today she had gone into Melodyland to look over the records, and there at the sales desk was a young woman listening to music on a Walkman. Miss Ormsby had seen other young people going about the streets with earphones on their heads. Where did the music come from anyway, and what did it feel like to be wired up in that fashion? At the sales desk of Melodyland Miss Ormsby had asked to be plugged in, and at once was delighted to be surrounded by music. She bought several tapes too, spending far more than she should have done and without regrets.

Now as she opened the glass door of Sunset Manor, she was met by a blast of hot dry air. They kept the temperature at a ridiculously high level. It was unhealthy. Or so thought Miss Ormsby who was used to wearing sweaters indoors. Hurrying along the hallway towards her was Arthur Wilkie. The old man had an arid peevish look about him. Miss Ormsby lay her parcels on a desk by the entrance and removed her green tam. She also switched off the Beethoven and greeted her former colleague, who stopped at once and gave her a sharp look.

"Oh!" he began and faltered. "It's you, Miss Ormsby."

"Arthur, how are you?" said Miss Ormsby. She took off the yellow earpieces. "Don't think me a complete fool, Arthur, but I have just bought one of these things, and let me tell you they're wonderful. Why you could listen to a symphony or learn a foreign language while you're out walking . . . ."

Arthur Wilkie stared at her a little wildly. "It's an outrage and there is no other word for it," he said. "How can we be expected to sustain an acceptable level of health on sandwiches and cheap, nasty little cakes?" He looked around the hallway. "I have a good mind to inform the authorities, Miss Ormsby. I suspect they will be interested to learn about this. Nor would I rule out a letter to the newspaper! I think the people of this town might like to hear about how the elderly are treated in this place."

Mr. Wilkie turned at once and mounted the stairs, supported by the railing, but climbing briskly enough, as would a man with a purpose. Watching him, Miss Ormsby concluded that the years had not dealt kindly with Arthur Wilkie.

NINE

"**Y**ou smell funny, Great-gramps," said Jason Truscott, who was six years old.

"So do you, you little peckerhead," said Lorne Truscott, who was seated on the sofa and laughing as he held his great-grandson at arms' length. The boy was aiming a kick at Lorne's genitals, though all in good-natured fun.

"You're a peckerhead," repeated Jason Truscott.

His sister, a solemn little girl of eight, sat on the floor of the Sun Room and stared at the television. Lorne had turned on a cartoon show for her.

The Sun Room was empty in the late afternoon; all the residents had gone to their rooms, evidently fatigued by the exertions of the Christmas tree party. Supper was still an hour away. Beyond the windows, the parking lot was deserted and in shadows from the winter sun that had now almost set behind the Woolco building in the shopping plaza across Transit Road. The snow was banked in the corners of the parking lot. Jason Truscott and his great-grandfather continued to tug at one another's arms in front of the sofa. "You're an old peckerhead, Great-gramps," said Jason.

Seated next to Lorne, the boy's mother lit another cigarette. She was using a soft drink can for an ashtray.

119

You weren't supposed to smoke in the Sun Room, and Lorne was glad that old Lucas wasn't around to report him. You could bet your ass she'd tell Rawlings, and then there'd be hell to pay. Rhonda smoked like a goddamn fiend and Lorne wished he could have seen her and the kids in his room. But his TV was on the blink and the kids had to have their television when they came to see him. Without the goddamn TV, they'd be climbing the walls. The little boy now managed to wrest free an arm and deliver a blow to Lorne's chest. It stung but Lorne only laughed. "You little bugger!" he cried.

The boy's mother, however, had had enough; this could be seen in the pale blue eyes that now regarded her son with impatience.

"All right, Jason," she said, "that's enough. Knock it off! Watch some TV with your sister." She sounded tired, but there was an edge to her voice that suggested a cuff on the ear was not far away. Unwilling to yield so easily, the boy continued to struggle in Lorne's grasp, though now and again he shot a wary glance at his mother.

"Jason," she said. "I'll give you the lickin' of your life if you don't lay off." The boy gave a final tug. "You're an old peckerhead, Great-gramps," he said. "And you smell funny." He abruptly giggled and sinking to the floor was soon absorbed in the cartoon show.

Lorne guessed that his granddaughter had come for money. He didn't like to admit it, but the truth was that she only brought the kids around when she wanted to put the bite on him for twenty or thirty dollars. Since that husband of hers walked out, they were always broke. Not that the son of a bitch had ever been much good in the money-making department. The trouble was that Rhonda knew bugger all about handling money. He could see that when he lived with them. First of the month when the cheque came in, it was all hunky-dory with video movies and beer and pizzas delivered to the door at all hours of the day and night. Then by the middle of the Christly month, they were eating Kraft dinners and scrounging around for pop bottles to take back to the store.

She didn't look after the kids right either. Holes in their socks! Christ Almighty, you'd think a woman could find a pair of socks without holes when she took the kids out visiting people. And their ears were dirty too. There was gum in their eyes, and that could only mean they hadn't had their faces washed. The Christly woman did nothing all day, but sit around watching the television and smoking cigarettes. The kids looked scrawny and washed-out too. Not that any Truscott had ever exactly been fat; they were all built thin and wiry. Around the house on Dock Street in the summertime they used to run around half-naked. Looked like a bunch of goddamn Indians. The whole house used to stink of dirty feet. Sometimes the girls complained. Velma was the fussy one. She used to get after Jack and Ernie, but they just laughed at her. One time Velma broke one of the boy's arms. They were playing out in the backyard and she twisted it up behind his back and snapped the son of a bitch. Old Man Holt took them up to the hospital in his Model A.

When Lorne glanced sideways at his granddaughter, he could see that she was out of sorts today. She looked surly as she smoked and watched the cartoon show. He wondered if it was her monthlies or maybe man trouble. She was seeing this new fellow, the truck driver. What the hell was his name? As he looked at Rhonda, he could see that she was a lot like her grandmother. Cassie hadn't been any great shakes either when it came to looking after the kids. All winter they coughed and had runny noses. In the summer there were stys and impetigo. You put that yellow stuff on the impetigo. What the hell was it called?

Lorne rummaged in his memory for the name of the salve. It had a sickly sweet smell to it. Like rotting flowers or something. What the hell was it called? It seemed to him

121

that if he could remember the name of the stuff, the kitchen on Dock Street would be there in the Sun Room with him: he would see his skinny pale children in their short pants and rubber boots; he would see the chipped plates and the linoleum and the wooden chairs and the old McClary stove. In the fading afternoon light Lorne looked at his granddaughter. She resembled Billy from the side, the way her face kind of rounded out. The little girl was like that too. And they both had Billy's pale colour and blond hair. The boy was dark like his half-breed father.

The kids were now laughing at the cartoon show, and even his granddaughter produced a bitter little smile at the antics of the cat and mouse. Christ Almighty, thought Lorne, they were around years ago at the Capitol Theatre. He and Cassie sometimes used to go to the show on Saturdays nights. They had cowboy movies on Saturday nights. Hopalong Cassidy. Lash Larue. Johnny Mack Brown. They had the cat and the mouse too and the Three Stooges and sometimes the fat and skinny guys. He used to fall asleep from the beer halfway through the evening.

Lorne asked Rhonda about her new boyfriend, and without taking her eyes off the television, she told him that Randy was a truck driver who lived in Barrie. They could only see one another now and then, but they were in love. This was the real thing. Randy hauled stuff between Toronto and Coteau Landing. He made a good wage. His wife was a bitch and wouldn't let go. They had kids. It was complicated. Listening to all this, Lorne tried to remember how old Rhonda was. Twenty-seven? Twenty-eight? He'd lost track of how many men had shifted in with her since the half-breed left. She seemed to like her tail, but then what Truscott didn't? He'd liked it enough himself at one time.

There were always girls hanging around the hockey team. He and Johnny Lalonde used to bang the bejesus out of some of them. They used that little storage room in the northwest corner of the old rink. It was filled with all kinds of junk, and they used to screw the girls on an old dusty mattress. There were any number of old pictures in that little room. He could remember one that he always faced when he was banging one of the girls. It was an old brown picture of a bunch of men standing around a steam engine in Begg's lumberyard. It was winter, because there was snow on the ground and the men wore overcoats with fur collars and derby hats. The picture had something to do with the railway coming to Moreton. He used to count those old bearded geezers when he was on top of Nellie Smith or one of the others.

When he moved into Sunset Manor three years ago, Nellie Smith was living on the third floor. One day he asked her if she could remember those days in the little storage room in the old rink. But Nellie had turned high and mighty. "I don't believe I do, Lorne," she said, looking at him as if he were a dog turd on the street. "And anyway," she said, "them days is all in the past." She was all dressed up like the Christmas goose and hanging around with a bunch of women from the Presbyterian Church. But that didn't matter. You can't change the past and he could remember when she was giving it to every guy on the hockey team. Poor old Nellie! Dead a year later from cancer.

Rhonda was talking about the Welfare people and how they were bugging her. Lorne could see that. They had different names nowadays, but they were the same assholes who used to bother him and Cassie after they laid him off at the Foundry. In those days the assholes worked for the Relief. You had to be an asshole to work for the Relief. Spying on you in the grocery store to see if you'd bought a package of chewing gum or some tobacco. Same bunch now, only they call themselves Welfare. With Christmas coming on and the kids looking for presents and stuff, Rhonda was wondering if he could manage fifty dollars.

His December cheque had come early and was up in his room uncashed. But fifty dollars! Holy Jesus, that was a lot of money! It was a good thing he'd got a few bucks from the house and had salted it away. He had twenty-five dollars in his purse and he told his granddaughter that he could manage that. Rhonda's face took on a pinched look when she didn't get what she wanted. Lorne could remember Billy looking exactly the same when he couldn't get the skates or the stick he asked for. It was a corker how something like the expression on a face could pass on down through the family.

The fire in his backside had started up again and Lorne guessed he was in for a bad night. Leaning forward he suddenly grabbed the boy by the ears. "Where in the world did you get a pair of ears like this? All sticking out and looking funny?" The boy scrambled to his feet ready and eager for more combat. But Lorne held his arms. "Whoa now, peckerhead! What do you say we all go over to The Chicken House for supper? It's my treat."

*   *   *

My heart is like a singing bird
Whose nest is in a watered shoot
My heart is like an apple tree
Whose boughs are bent with thick-set fruit

Miss Ormsby sipped some Johnny Walker and screwed shut an eye that was watering from the smoke curling up from the cigarette in her mouth. She was not reading verse aloud tonight. There was no purchase in awakening the elephant next door. She removed the cigarette from her mouth.

Raise me a dais of silk and down
Hang it with vair and purple dyes
Carve it in doves and pomengrates
And peacocks with a hundred eyes;

124

Miss Ormsby lingered over Christina Rossetti's ornate words. Allan Webb had once explained the meaning of vair to her in his overheated classroom. Vair, he told her, standing by the window, was squirrel fur used by the nobility during the Middle Ages as a lining for heraldic garments. Allan, bless him, knew about things like vair. And such words appeared so magical on March afternoons when it seemed always to be snowing. Allan was sick of the winter. The weather had made him plaintive. In Devon, he reminded her, it would now be spring; there would be fields of flowers and grass and spring lambs. Yet in this godforsaken Ontario town the snow persisted. Day after day it fell from dark gray skies. It was *too* depressing. Even when he complained, however, she loved to listen to his soft Devon accent.

Everyone else had gone home. They could faintly hear the shouts from the basketball practice in the gymnasium. In the halls Mr. Proulx pushed his broom through the Dustbane. Miss Ormsby was thirty-one years old, a tall plain red-headed woman. That year, to her father's amazement, she had tried to accommodate the fashion of the day by trying a new hairstyle. In the last year of the war, women arranged their hair into a heavy mantle that covered the back of their necks. But Miss Ormsby soon discovered that her hair lacked the texture for such a style; it was far too thin and brittle. And so finally she had it cut into the familiar bowl and bangs. As someone put it, you couldn't pass a penny for a crown.

Allan wore his English suits and jackets to school and his clothes seemed altogether strange to staff and pupils alike at Moreton District High School. Miss Ormsby, however, thought he looked dapper and refined in his belted coats and English leather shoes. His face was delicate and girlish; she imagined Shelley looking something like Allan Webb. Over his high polished brow rode a shock of blond hair that was stiff and ribbed like sea sand. His eyes were alert and scornful and he made enemies with his manner. He *was* a sarcastic young man; one certainly couldn't deny that. Some called him little Lord Webb, and Arthur Wilkie was among those who were happy enough to see him fall.

All winter Miss Ormsby and Allan Webb read poetry together after classes. In the spring they took walks in the park or in the woods by the edge of the lake, stepping carefully over the sodden dirt. Amid the patches of rotting snow were violets and trilliums, hepaticas and jack-in-the-pulpits. He was delighted when she showed him these flowers from the Ontario woods. He talked about his childhood and the boarding school he had attended and his parents and his older brother who was in the Air Force. Allan said he had a heart condition that kept him out of the service. He talked also about the poems and novels that he would write one day. While he talked, he pushed his fingers through that pale wiry hair.

On Sunday afternoons he came to the house on Park Street, and together they listened to Chopin and Liszt, sitting wordlessly in the parlour that smelled of old lemon oil. The windows to the verandah were open, and as the sun travelled westward, its light on the leaves of Dutchman's Pipe entered the room, casting a soft brightness over the dark wood. The old 78's, spinning fiercely on the turntable, poured forth sonatas and mazurkas. Sometimes Allan dozed and she would study his face with its pale skin and eyelashes the colour of sand, the long straight nose and imposing brow. He always stayed for supper, and he and Miss Ormsby's father would talk about the hypocrisy of organized religion. Allan's father was a rector in Barnstaple and there had been a serious family quarrel over religion. This had something to do with his being in Canada, but details were never forthcoming. Miss Ormsby's father, however, was sympathetic. Later they all sat in the kitchen and listened to Edgar Bergen and Charlie McCarthy.

When the scandal broke, Mr. Pigeon gave him only twenty-four hours to get out of town before criminal charges would be laid. The young man at the Y.M.C.A. was, it seems, a minor. Allan came around to see her the night before he left. He sat on the steps of the verandah and smoked, leaning forward with his elbows on his knees.

"I've been rather naughty, Kay," he said. "And I don't think your little town is quite ready to acknowledge certain kinds of behaviour. Mind you, it wouldn't surprise me if there's more of it going on than the good folks would like to admit."

From her chair in the darkness she could see only his pale face and the burning cigarette. She hated him briefly for this casual sundering of their friendship. He sounded far too buoyant to suit her. It was almost as if this incident had provided him with the excuse to escape. What had taken place in the Y.M.C.A. locker room was all a mystery to her. She knew nothing of these matters and wished only that such events were not allowed to interfere with more important things in life. She would miss the poetry and his companionship on Sunday afternoons in the green restful light of the little parlour.

It all happened during the week the war ended in Europe. Allan took the bus to Toronto on VE Day and his presence was soon forgotten. The town was happily distracted by the news from Europe. That night her father walked downtown to watch the parade, but she stayed at home, sitting on the verandah in the May evening. She could hear the band music and the cheering as it came across the trees from King Street. Boys were lighting bonfires in the park, and there were sirens and the smell of grass smoke in the air. She sat on the verandah thinking of Allan Webb on the bus to Toronto.

They promised to keep in touch and for a few years she

did receive letters from him. There were several from Toronto, where he was working for a department store. Then they came postmarked from Vancouver, where he was a supply teacher. Later he worked there for the CBC. Then came a postcard from Vancouver Island, where he was writing something. He mentioned a friend named Jimmy. It was odd that she should or could remember such a detail. Two or three years later she received a Christmas card from England. He was now looking after his widowed mother in Exeter. They took holidays together in Cornwall, and now and then, there were postcards from Penzance with pictures of the seaside hotel they favoured each summer. The hotel had a long verandah that faced the sea. There were tables and chairs of wicker and waiters in white jackets.

Towards the end of the fifties, the postcards stopped. It was as if Allan had ceased to exist and perhaps that was true; he may have died early, poor man. Sometimes, however, people merely lose interest in old acquaintances. It becomes a burden to keep in touch. Each year the Christmas card list grows more and more unwieldy, and so a decision is made and a name is struck off. Allan would now only be in his late sixties, and Miss Ormsby liked to think that she could see him in the hotel in Penzance. He was the sharp-tongued elderly man in the wicker chair on the long verandah that overlooked the sea. Did he ever think of his winter in Moreton, Ontario, during the last year of the war? Miss Ormsby wondered, too, if he had ever published a book? Now and then she looked up his name in *Books in Print* in the library. There were several namesakes listed, but she doubted that he was one of the authors.

Miss Ormsby stared at the poetry book in her lap. She felt suddenly sleepy and old. To take off her clothes and put on her nightgown seemed like an ordeal past enduring. She missed her bedroom on Park Street. "Don't be such a foolish old thing," she whispered.

For most of the evening Mr. Wilkie had been working on his letter about the sandwiches and cakes. His efforts, however, had failed to satisfy him; the letter didn't sound quite right. Working with words always excited and angered him. Words were too elusive and imprecise, and Mr. Wilkie preferred numbers, which plainly said that this was so and that was that. Words on the other hand seemed like snares designed to entrap you. Ada had written all the letters in their household. There was the time that the ceiling in the apartment on Queen Street collapsed; Ada responded to that by writing a two-page letter to the landlord expressing general outrage and the need for compensation. There had once been a fuss with a local car dealer too. The man wasn't prepared to honour the terms of the warranty, and so Ada wrote their head office.

Women were better with words than men, thought Mr. Wilkie in his chair by the window. It was the way their minds worked. They were good at manipulating words and that was why they were running so many things nowadays. You had only to look at the notice board downstairs to see who was chairing the various clubs and committees. And who was in the administrator's office if it wasn't a woman? And look at those feminist people in the population at large? Such people had infiltrated governments at all levels.

Mr. Wilkie heard the screeching of brakes and waited for the sound of rending metal. When he arose to peer out the window, however, he could see no accident. It had only been a driver braking sharply for the traffic light. It wasn't like the time the bread van overturned after it collided with the dump truck coming out of the shopping plaza. That was something to see; there were buns and cakes all over the road. Mr. Wilkie sat down and again began his letter, carefully underlining the first few words. *To whom it may concern!*

At three o'clock Lorne Truscott got up again and went to the bathroom. It was already his fourth trip of the night. Standing over the toilet he passed another few drops of water. It was vexing. The goddamn thing just didn't work anymore, and you couldn't get a new one. At least he hadn't heard that you could, though with all this transplant stuff going on, maybe it was only a question of time before they could outfit a man with a new dong. Well, when that day arrived, he vowed to be the first in line. Lorne noisily cleared his throat and spat into the bowl. That might wake her up; he knew she hated the sound. Next he flushed the toilet and coughed more than was strictly necessary before returning to bed.

TEN

In Drug World Mrs. Lucas was looking at plastic bottles of rat poison. The print on the labels was so small that she had to hold the containers at arm's length to read the instructions. Behind the counter, the pharmacist, a balding middle-aged man, watched her. He suspected that she was from the retirement home across Transit Road. Most of the old people who came into his store lived there and a few of them bore watching. Now and then one would slip an item into pocket or handbag. The pharmacist wondered why the stout old woman was interested in rat poison. Surely conditions in the place weren't that bad, though from time to time one read dismal stories in the newspapers about how the elderly lived.

For some time now the pharmacist and his wife had been puzzling over what to do with her father, who was living with them. The old man, however, was growing more difficult with each passing day, and they had in fact considered putting his name on the list for the place across the road. But if the residents had to deal with rats! It was a shame that people who had raised families and paid taxes all their lives should have to contend with vermin and rodents at the end of their days. The pharmacist felt himself growing indignant and passed a hand over the top of his head. The skin there was warm to the touch. The flesh in his cheeks had also darkened with blood. Perhaps in the circumstances a phone call or a letter to the Board of Health would not be amiss. The man stepped out from behind his counter and approached Mrs. Lucas, who was now inspecting the label on a package of Mouse Treat.

"Having a little problem with rodents, Madam?" asked the pharmacist. "Perhaps I may be of some assistance."

At his words, Mrs. Lucas was taken aback. It was her experience that nowadays store help didn't offer assistance; they let you muddle through on your own. You could spend half the morning in a place like this looking for corn plasters or milk of magnesia, and nobody would open his mouth to help. Yet here was this druggist staring down at her! Could he possibly divine her intentions? It seemed unlikely, but maybe you had to sign a paper if you bought poison. Maybe that was how they caught people. She thought she could remember a crime show on the television where the police tracked down a man who had poisoned his wife. They had traced him to the drug store where he'd bought the dope. "Do I have to sign anything if I buy this mouse seed?" asked Mrs. Lucas.

"That isn't necessary, Madam." The pharmacist smiled. "Do you have mice over in the Manor?"

Mrs. Lucas regarded him suspiciously. "What I got, I got," she said.

The pharmacist returned to his counter. The poor old scout was just like his father-in-law. They all get testy with age. Opening the phone book, he began to look for the number of the Board of Health. He could already feel his skin cooling down. Mrs. Lucas waited in the line-up at the check-out counter. It never failed. There was always a line-up, and only one cashier on duty when she wanted to buy something.

Mrs. Lucas had decided not to murder Lorne Truscott. Half the night she had lain awake and thought about it.

132

Once she even got up and consulted the Bible. There were cases in olden times when God allowed you to kill your enemies, but she couldn't find the appropriate passages. When she finally slept, she had a dream in which Pastor Bob stood in his pulpit and preached to her. She was the only one in his Church of Gold in California. He stood before her in his nice powder blue suit and he told her that killing people just didn't square with being a Christian, unless you were defending your country against the Communists or other infidels.

When she awoke from that dream, Mrs. Lucas decided that instead of killing Lorne Truscott, she would just make him good and sick. There surely couldn't be everlasting punishment if you just made someone deathly ill. In fact, if you looked at it in a certain way, you could see it as a lesson. She would teach him a thing or two about what lay in store for people who didn't know how to be good neighbours. If she could just make him sick enough to go to the hospital over Christmas, it would be a genuine blessing. She could then get Ward to talk to Mrs. Rawlings about changing rooms. Mrs. Lucas surmised that a little Mouse Treat would get the job done.

She moved forward in the lineup, taking a tabloid from the rack by the cash register. According to the headlines, there were UFOs around and about again. There had been another incident along the Maine-New Brunswick border. A family of four had been snatched away for an indeterminate period of time and then returned to earth. An account of this adventure lay within.

Miss Ormsby sat in an inspired state by the window. She was wired-up to her Walkman, listening to Chopin's "Revolutionary Etude." When the Winnebago pulled into the parking lot, she wondered how anyone could maneuver such a clumsy-looking rig over the icy roads. She had never even used her car in winter. From late November until April, the little gray bustle-backed Plymouth made in 1952 sat in the garage with the battery removed. George Scully always fixed it up for her. Now Miss Ormsby watched as a woman stepped down from the driver's side of the Winnebago. She looked sturdy enough in her trousers and heavy sweater. There was something familiar about her too; it was the way she stood, leaning into one hip as she waited for the man to climb down from the other side.

Miss Ormsby unhooked her Walkman and paid more attention. She could now see that the driver was her cousin Doreen. The man who was walking around the machine kicking at the tires was Doreen's husband, or rather her second husband. And here Miss Ormsby experienced a moment of panic. She felt suddenly dismantled by the bleak truth that, for the life of her, she could not remember the man's name. It had vanished from her memory. She had met him a half dozen times in the past two years, twice, in fact, in the last few months. She had entertained him in her home and remembered him vividly enough. He was considerably older than Doreen, a quiet friendly man who had retired early from some paper mill up north. But his name was nowhere to be found in Miss Ormsby's head.

It was monstrous for one's memory to behave like this. At such moments one could foresee only a slow decline into senility. Miss Ormsby breathed deeply. Doreen's first husband's name was Arthur Hopewell. That much was certain. Mr. and Mrs. Arthur Hopewell. She had sent Christmas cards to that name for fifteen years. Then three years ago Art died suddenly of a heart attack and Miss Ormsby went up to North Bay to the funeral. Doreen was in a terrible state; she wept through the entire ceremony. One might have thought that she would never recover from poor Art's death. Yet within a year she had married this man. *What was his name?* Miss Ormsby leaned forward and watched Doreen and her husband walk towards the front door.

She would have to see them in the Sun Room; there simply wasn't enough space to entertain people in her room, and in any case it was too cluttered and stale. It was just like Doreen to turn up unannounced; her mother had been the same. Suddenly at supper time Marion and her husband and Doreen would appear on the doorstep. They were just passing by and thought they'd drop in on cousin Kay. It was a scramble to find a meal for them, and they all sat like lumps in the kitchen watching your every move.

As a girl Doreen used to spend two weeks each summer in Moreton. Her mother put her on the bus from Toronto and Doreen would phone from the terminal. "I'm here, Aunty Kay." They were really second cousins, but because of the difference of nearly thirty-five years, Doreen always thought of Miss Ormsby as her aunt. Each summer Miss Ormsby reminded herself that it was a good idea to have a young person in the house. One who lived alone could become peculiar with solitary habits, and it was surely beneficial now and again to disrupt routine. Yet Doreen, a big girl who appeared always to be spilling out of her clothes, got on Miss Ormsby's nerves. She seemed constantly to be underfoot: when she wasn't traipsing around the house after you, she was watching television or sitting on the verandah surrounded by movie magazines and sticky bottles of Coca-Cola.

Miss Ormsby went into the tiny bathroom and ran a brush through her hair. This was Doreen's third visit to Moreton since the spring. Did she think that, with the stroke, her cousin was now about to expire and leave her worldly possessions to her? That was perhaps an uncharitable thought, but there was no denying that Doreen had an acquisitive eye in her head. When she visited in the summer, she had so coveted the little cherrywood secretary in the front hall, that finally Miss Ormsby told her to

135

take it. The little desk would no doubt have fetched a good price at the auction, but the avid look in Doreen's eyes was too painful to behold. And so Miss Ormsby had said, "Take it Doreen, and anything else you fancy."

The cherrywood secretary had been one of her parents' wedding gifts. In its little drawers and pigeonholes, Miss Ormsby had filed utility bills and grocery store coupons. The lid folded back to reveal a writing table, and on it she had made out her income tax and written cheques to the telephone people and the oil company. From there she had conducted the business of the household as her father had done before her. But after all, it was only a desk. When you left a house after seventy years, you had to get rid of things. Doreen, however, was sentimental about furniture and family connections. She had gushed over the secretary. "I'll always think of you, Aunty Kay, when I use it. We have to stick together you know. We're the only Ormsbys left."

That was not quite true. The family was never prolific and over the years had been depleted, but there were cousins from Uncle Everett's side out in Alberta. In a sense, however, Doreen was right; they were stuck with one another. When the telephone rang and Miss Crawley told her that she had visitors, Miss Ormsby had already splashed some lilac water on her throat and thrown a cardigan across her shoulders.

In the Sun Room several residents including Lorne Truscott had watched the arrival of the Winnebago. The presence of such a vehicle in the parking lot on a winter afternoon was a strange and wonderful event. Lorne got up from his chair by the TV where he had been watching a drama with Mrs. Huddle and Mrs. Somers. Walking to the window with his hands in his trouser pockets he exclaimed, "By Jesus, that's some rig! The whole shooting

match on wheels! You can eat, sleep, watch TV, take a
crap, anything you like, and you don't have to go near any
motel. After your day's driving, you just pull that thing
into one of them parks, plug her in, sit back, and have a
couple of drinks while your steak's frying. You don't have
to bother with restaurants or anything. It's all there under
one roof and on four wheels. That's the way to go, eh!"

He addressed these remarks to no one in particular,
but the slow wagging of heads suggested that some had
listened and agreed with Lorne's approval of life in a
motor home. The nearest person to him was Mrs. Fenerty.
The nurses had settled her in a chair by the window so that
she could enjoy the afternoon sun. She had been sleeping,
but Lorne's words, meaningless noise to Mrs. Fenerty,
awakened her. When she opened her eyes, she saw an odd
contraption on wheels and thought at once that it was
some kind of ambulance. Someone was about to be trans-
ported to the hospital; that happened now and again. The
man beside her, whom she could not identify, was talking
to her about palm trees in Florida. It was baffling, and for
a moment Mrs. Fenerty wondered in fact whether she was
awake at all or only dreaming. To assure herself of the
reality of things, she grasped the arm of her chair and
discovered that it was indeed a chair. The man beside her
kept talking, and Mrs. Fenerty wished that the nurses
would come and help her to her room. "You and me, Mrs.
F.," Lorne Truscott was saying. "I can see us going down
the highway in that rig. Heading for the palm trees and
the sandy beaches. Why living in that thing would take
twenty-five years off your life!"

Because he was looking out the window at the Winne-
bago, Lorne Truscott did not see Mrs. Lucas enter the Sun
Room. In her clenched hand was a vial that had once held
gall bladder pills; now, however, it was half-filled with
Mouse Treat. Mrs. Somers was fast asleep, and Mrs.
Huddle was too absorbed in the television drama to notice.

137

It was no trick then for Mrs. Lucas to empty the vial's contents into Lorne Truscott's tea. To the best of her knowledge, no one saw her do this.

"We can't stay long, Aunty Kay. We're just passing through on our way to Fort Lauderdale. We'd have left two weeks ago, but something went on the wagon. We had to order a part from Hamilton, and with the Christmas mail and everything, it just took ages to get to us." Doreen's voice carried down the hallway to the Sun Room, where the residents turned to watch Miss Ormsby escort her guests to chairs in a corner by the piano. The old folks leaned forward to listen; it was unusual to see strangers in the place during the week.

Miss Ormsby had been hoping that Doreen would mention her husband's name. In his quiet, gallant way, the man had lightly gripped Miss Ormsby by the elbows and kissed her cheek at the front door. But familiarity had been assumed and no names were forthcoming. Now he sat beside Doreen, a polite stranger humouring his new wife's whim to visit an old relative. He was a compact gray-haired man who looked to have a number of years on Doreen. She seemed to prefer older men. Arthur Hope-well had been at least ten years older, and this man had to be close to sixty. *What was his name?* Miss Ormsby searched the mild eager face for a clue. What if she had to introduce them to someone?

She felt a flutter in her chest at the thought and nodded, listening to Doreen's braying voice. "This is very nice, Aunty Kay," said Doreen, rotating her thick neck to survey the Sun Room. "Very nice," she repeated, smooth-ing a hand over the chair as if assessing the value of the fabric. "Of course it's not like your own home. I imagine you must miss it after all those years."

Doreen still seemed to fill her clothes to bursting. A

certain lewdness prevailed in the large bosom and the swelling thighs; the heavy trousered bottom suggested coarseness. Miss Ormsby herself was innocent of the ways of the flesh, but she could detect lubricity. She hadn't spent forty years in a high school classroom without being able to recognize female vulgarity. There were always those girls whose instincts for mating were abundantly evident in the way they carried themselves. Miss Ormsby could remember Doreen lounging in shorts on the verandah on Park Street. There was something of her grandfather in her; a strong hint of the man who had smelled of bay rum and tobacco and who had pressed himself against Miss Ormsby in the raspberry canes on a summer morning long ago.

Doreen was asking about the meals at Sunset Manor when the old man in the baseball cap finished his tea and crossed the room towards them. Someone had told Miss Ormsby that the old man's name was Truscott. There had been Truscotts in her classroom over the years and they were no lovers of literature. She doubted whether any of them had gone further than Grade Ten. She remembered them as a lawless tribe who lived down on Dock Street. And this jaunty old gaffer still looked full of mischief. He stood by their chairs with his hands in his pockets, rocking on his heels. "That your rig out there, Mister?" he asked.

Doreen's husband looked up and sprang to his feet as though delighted to find male company. "Why yes," he said, sticking out a hand. "Ed Leitch from Kapuskasing. The wife and me are on the way to Florida. Just dropped in on our aunt here." Ed Leitch inclined his head towards Miss Ormsby. Ed Leitch! Of course! She would write down the name the minute she got back to her room. Doreen was shaking hands with Lorne Truscott who had introduced himself. "How are you today, Lorne?"

"Fit as a fiddle with all the strings attached," said Lorne.

Doreen's laughter was expansive and hearty, but Miss Ormsby felt a little faint with tiredness. The burden of remembering Ed Leitch's name weighed on her heart. She wished they would go, but the three of them were chattering on like old acquaintances. Truscott was a joker, and Miss Ormsby could now remember her father mentioning from time to time what a damn fool this Truscott was. He was always pulling practical jokes, and his antics sometimes endangered men's lives on the floor of the Foundry. He was, she believed, eventually let go. At something Truscott said, Doreen showed her large teeth in laughter. She enjoyed the rough companionship of men; their leering stories pleased her. The old man was trying to finagle a visit to the motor home, but Ed Leitch was sensible enough to realize that once inside, they'd never get rid of him.

It finally came time for them to leave and Doreen made a fuss, squeezing Miss Ormsby's hand and pressing a small Christmas package on her. "We won't be seeing you until April, Aunty Kay, but I'll write now and then. I'll let you know what we're doing. I want you to please take care of yourself. I put our address inside your present, and as soon as we get a phone number, we'll pass it along. Dear Aunty Kay," she repeated. There were tears in her eyes for Heaven's sake. Laughter one minute and tears the next. Off and on like the kitchen tap. That was Doreen for you.

Like a member of the family Lorne Truscott followed them to the front door and waved goodbye. After the Leitch's left, he turned to Miss Ormsby. "What did you say your name was?" He seemed to have lost his good humour and now sounded peevish and out of sorts.

"Ormsby. Kay Ormsby."

"There used to be an Ormsby at the Foundry. He worked in the office."

"That was my father," said Miss Ormsby. "He was the bookkeeper."

"Is that right?" said Lorne Truscott. "I remember him. I always found him kind of stuck-up."

In the Sun Room Mrs. Lucas watched the nurses help Mrs. Fenerty with her walking frame. It took the old woman ten minutes to get clear of the room, and every second was a thorn in the flesh for Mrs. Lucas. She felt like shouting wild words every time she observed Mrs. Fenerty in motion. To calm herself Mrs. Lucas reflected on the afternoon's events; on the whole, she had found them pleasing.

To begin with, she had got close enough in the light to see that her neighbour's hair was real. The woman did not wear a wig after all, and that was a mercy. Although she couldn't exactly say why, the notion of living next to a bald-headed woman had been oddly unsettling for Mrs. Lucas. In the second place, Truscott had drunk his tea without noticing anything. Mrs. Lucas had watched him with satisfaction in every fibre of her being. It was true that so far there were no effects from the potion and he was still as obnoxious as ever. Going over to those people from the motor home and making a nuisance of himself. But there was always tomorrow, and somehow she would contrive to give him another portion of the seeds. The whole enterprise, she concluded, was lending shape and purpose to her existence. Now, with Mrs. Fenerty out of sight at last, Mrs. Lucas was feeling, for the moment at least, quite contented with life in general.

ELEVEN

Mrs. Rawlings's heart was ablaze with hatred and resentment, though all was concealed by the smile she directed across her desk at the young woman from the Health Board. A Ms. Patricia Venables was writing in her report book, and Mrs. Rawlings watched, the fingers of her right hand drumming along the desk top. Her left hand, now fashioned into an immense fist, lay at the ready in her lap. Because of this business, she was missing an important meeting of the Christmas Concert Committee.

There was an enemy in her midst. These allegations of rats and malnutrition were the handiwork of some malcontent, and Mrs. Rawlings suspected Edna Lucas. The woman obviously bore a grudge because her request for a room change had been denied. It was likely that she was the person who had telephoned the Health Board with this wild talk of rodents and cold, unsatisfactory lunches. It was maddening to have to listen to such stuff; moreover, Ms. Venables's perusal of the menu and her inspection of the premises had revealed nothing untoward except a faulty burner on one of the stoves in the kitchen. "That burner will have to be mended within thirty days," instructed Ms. Venables in her soft, precise voice. The woman came, by God, from some island in the Caribbean and was as black as your shoe. Such people were crowding into the country and they were *all* working for the government.

Mrs. Rawlings watched Ms. Venables writing in her report book and decided to try again. "I must reiterate, Ms. Venables, that I consider it highly unfair and inappropriate to inspect Sunset Manor on the basis of anonymous telephone calls. Perhaps if the caller had identified himself or herself, we could find out just what lies behind these absurd accusations."

Ms. Venables looked up unsmiling, her dark polished brow a plane of ebony. "As an experienced administrator, Mrs. Rawlings, you must know that the Board is under no obligation to give you advance warning of visits. Indeed, it could be argued that to do so would be to defeat the purpose of these periodic inspections." She consulted her book. "I see, for instance, that Sunset Manor was down for a December inspection in any case. These calls came in when they did, but I shouldn't make too much of them if I were you. The bottom line is that your residence appears to meet the standards established by the Ministry."

"I never doubted that for a particle of a second, Ms. Venables," said Mrs. Rawlings with an edge to her voice.

"Except, of course, for that stove burner," said Ms. Venables. "I shall be returning within thirty days to look at that. I expect you'll see to it in the next little while."

"Have no fear on that score," said Mrs. Rawlings, who longed for a time when station and custom might have allowed her to hurl this young woman across the room.

Ms. Venables had now put her writing materials into a briefcase and stood up. "Can you not at least," asked Mrs. Rawlings, "tell me whether the caller or callers were male or female?"

"I can't see what possible difference that would make, Mrs. Rawlings," said Ms. Venables, drawing on gloves. "The calls themselves were unimportant. What matters is the condition of your residence, and our concern for the safety and well-being of your patrons."

"Splendid," said Mrs. Rawlings emerging from behind her desk, but clasping her hands at the back lest they find their way around Ms. Venables's throat. "Thank you so very much for your trouble, and may I offer you the compliments of the season."

"Thank you," said Ms. Venables. "And you will remember the stove burner?"

"Depend upon it," said Mrs. Rawlings, showing the young woman to the door. Shortly thereafter Mrs. Rawlings cancelled all appointments and left for the morning.

He must, thought Mrs. Lucas, have the gizzard of an ostrich. The residents of Sunset Manor, festive in party hats strapped to their chins, were singing Christmas carols in the dining hall after lunch. Holding the song sheet away from her, Mrs. Lucas opened and closed her mouth, producing a kind of whispered response. At the next table Lorne Truscott sang loudly, but he was confusing anyone within earshot by mangling the words. The man was obviously intoxicated.

Mrs. Lucas had hoped to dose his cornflakes at breakfast, but that had proved too difficult. By the greatest good fortune, however, the kitchen staff had served up a soup of beans and lentils for luncheon, a concoction that easily disguised any foreign substance. With her tray Mrs. Lucas had stood behind Lorne Truscott in the line-up by the steam tables. When he had reached for the rolls, it had been child's play to administer the treatment.

To her dismay, however, Truscott had spooned up the soup with no apparent ill effects. In his uncouth way, he had even brought the bowl to his mouth to empty the dregs. By now Mrs. Lucas had hoped to see him collapsed and writhing on the floor; instead he was grinning at one and all while he sang his ridiculous words.

While shepherds washed their socks by night!

Sacrilegious old goat, thought Mrs. Lucas, feeling a rumble or two in her own digestive tract. The beans and lentils were already about their business, singing their own dismal tune.

M r. Wilkie had hastened away from the festivities in the dining hall and gained the safety of his room. He now sat in his chair by the window, panting and fearful for his heart. He had moved along the hallway faster than a man of his years ought perhaps to have done. He also felt a little faint with hunger, having eaten only a roll at lunch. The paramount question now was survival. It no longer merely had to do with cold lunches and inadequate nutrition; it had now become a matter of the most funda-mental urgency. Nor would they allow you to bring food into your room; supposedly it attracted vermin. Very well then, but how was one to survive? "Answer me that?" asked Mr. Wilkie aloud, stirring uneasily in his chair.

He had seen the fat woman put something into Trus-cott's soup. It was quite obvious that a conspiracy was afoot. Who was to say that his own meal had not been similarly tampered with? Clearly they were planning to eliminate all the men in the Manor. Not satisfied with the fact that they already outnumbered men sixty-one to thirty-three, they were now intent on having the place entirely to themselves. They would not be happy until all the men were dead and buried. Then who knows what might go on under this roof? In the farthest reaches of Mr. Wilkie's mind fluttered images of old barefoot women in white gowns dancing beneath the moon. Some were performing strange rituals by candlelight. All were celebrating their dominion over men.

Mr. Wilkie felt a bitter sense of futility. His telephone call to the Board of Health had only brought a woman to the place. He had seen her in the hallway talking to Cora Rawlings. In the circumstances, only a fool could anticipate reform. The female of the species, Mr. Wilkie decided, reached its ideal state of development at about sixteen years. Afterwards, they became nothing more than a nuisance and then eventually a threat to one's very existence.

In his chair Mr. Wilkie remembered the girls in his classroom: the saddle shoes and socks, the pretty bare legs, the plaid skirts and angora sweaters. When he bent across their desks to move a decimal point, he could smell their hair. Sometimes his arm brushed a breast. The poor things were always so grateful to pass. It was an everlasting pity that they grew up to plot against your life. Mr. Wilkie turned to his puzzle book. A vegetable marrow was said to weigh nine-tenths of its weight plus nine-tenths of a pound. Determine the weight of the marrow. The problem was simplicity itself, and as he worked it out, Mr. Wilkie considered the other matter. Perhaps it *was* now time to involve the police.

Mrs. Rawlings parked her car by the side of the road and tramped through the snow into the woods. Clenching her fists and turning her face heavenward, she began to scream. Her cries rang out in the cold, still air, and birds and small forest creatures, fearing an imminent skirmish with death, started at once. A great horned owl awakened and took flight, while the dry trees quivered and hummed like immense tuning forks.

TWELVE

Seated on a stool next to the examining table Miss Ormsby awaited the doctor. She could hear the murmur of voices from the room next door where Dr. Carswell was examining another patient. In her faded organdy slip, Miss Ormsby felt vulnerable and old. There was no gainsaying what time demanded of flesh and bone. A moment before she had studied herself in the small mirror on the wall. Her pale freckled shoulders and arms looked as brittle as old plaster. An ancient ruin am I, she thought, making a face at the mirror to examine her teeth. They were still her own, though discoloured and fragile. Now and then old fillings gave way and crumbled to bits; sometimes in the mornings she awakened to mysterious aches travelling along her jawline. A ruin in body perhaps but not, she hoped, in mind.

She was, however, growing doubtful about that too, and wondered whether she should tell the doctor about these tiresome spells of forgetfulness. At lunch today, for instance, she was approached by a Mrs. Featherstone. Suddenly in the noisy dining hall, there appeared before her this huge smiling face asking why Miss Ormsby had not attended the Great Books Club meeting this morning. Apparently, at some point during the past week, Miss

Ormsby had accepted membership in the Great Books Club and agreed to attend its meetings. She was appalled by Mrs. Featherstone's inquiry, for she had utterly forgotten. Letheward is this frail craft bound, thought Miss Ormsby staring at Mrs. Featherstone's huge amiable face. Mrs. Featherstone, however, had been good about it, patting Miss Ormsby's arm and assuring her that all was forgiven. After she left, Miss Ormsby jotted down her name in her notebook. Mrs. Featherstone! An odd name. Oxymoronic. Mrs. Oxymoron!

Now Miss Ormsby wondered whether Dr. Carswell would want to know of these lapses. The truth was that she did not feel comfortable with the young doctor whom she had seen only a half dozen times since the stroke. Before that she had not seen a doctor in twenty-five years. Old Dr. McAlister had been the family physician, but the Ormsbys had seldom used him. In times past people didn't run to doctors for every little ache and pain. She could count on the fingers of one hand the visits Dr. McAlister had made to the house on Park Street.

Miss Ormsby looked up as Dr. Carswell came into the room. He was a hearty young man with a head of vigorous, bushy hair and he was dressed for July in slacks and short-sleeved shirt. The hair on his short, powerful arms looked as soft and thick as fur. He was built like a football player, though the large head with its turbulent hair put Miss Ormsby more in mind of Beethoven. The doctor was holding a clipboard and smiling. "And how are we today, Miss Ormsby?"

"We are fine, Dr. Carswell," replied Miss Ormsby. If he noticed the sarcasm, he didn't let on; instead he settled himself in the chair opposite her and consulted his clipboard. "So how are you feeling in general?"

"I'm alright," said Miss Ormsby.

"Staying on your medication?"

"Yes," she lied. In fact, she frequently forgot to take the pills; taking pills had never been a part of her life.

"It's very important that you don't neglect your medication," said Dr. Carswell fiddling with the blood pressure apparatus. "Now let's have a look at your BP, shall we?"

His meaty-looking hands, their knuckles covered with hair, were soft and warm. He wrapped the cuff around her pale arm and pumped the little rubber ball. Miss Ormsby watched the column of mercury rise and fall. Dr. Carswell frowned. "It's still a little on the high side," he said. "I wish I could persuade you to give up cigarettes."

Miss Ormsby said nothing while the doctor unwrapped the cuff. "I have patients older than you who have quit," he said.

"Why?" asked Miss Ormsby.

"Why what?"

"Why have they quit smoking in their seventies and eighties?"

Dr. Carswell laughed. "Why, it makes them feel better! They breathe more easily. Their blood pressure falls. Their heart rate drops. They probably prolong their lives." He playfully rapped Miss Ormsby's knee with his hairy knuckles.

"Hey, smoking ain't good for you, lady!"

"But I enjoy it," said Miss Ormsby. "Why give up habits that one enjoys when one is near the end of life?"

Dr. Carswell leaned back and crossed his arms, looking at her with a kind of grave smirk. "Come on now, the end of life? What kind of talk is that? If you take care of yourself, there is no reason . . ."

"Why I should ever die?" interrupted Miss Ormsby. "But I surely must one day, Dr. Carswell. And soon, relatively speaking of course."

Miss Ormsby shifted her bony bottom on the stool. "I am now in my seventy-fifth year, Doctor. That in itself is a pretty good span, and I'm immensely grateful to whomever, the gods perhaps, my genes, for the time I've been allowed. I have lasted longer than my father and a good deal longer than my poor mother. There is little evidence on either side of my parents' families that members lived on into their eighties or nineties. Nor, when I think of it, would I have any wish to do so. And so it comes to this, does it not? I probably have, at the most, five years. That's sixty months and counting. Under the circumstances, why should I not continue to indulge in those little pleasures that bring comfort and relief from the daily round and the common task?"

Dr. Carswell was grinning at her. "What's all this talk of death, Miss Ormsby? Why be so morbid?"

"On the contrary," said Miss Ormsby, "I consider it morbid not to think of death. Only by thinking of death can one come to value and enjoy life. After all, it's only a brief feast that we partake of is it not? How did the great man put it?

> *We are such stuff*
> *As dreams are made on, and our little life*
> *Is rounded with a sleep.*

"Prospero." She smiled. "*The Tempest*." She was back in the classroom. Once a teacher, always a teacher!

Dr. Carswell seemed confounded by her. He wagged his big head of unruly hair. "You are something, Miss Ormsby. You are really something. Now let's have a listen to that ticker of yours."

Bending down, he placed the stethoscope against her chest; his great bushy head was mere inches from her face and she could hear his steady breathing. All business now, he moved around, thumping her back with strong fingers. This talk of death had undermined his essential jollity. She supposed that doctors felt uneasy about the subject. After all, their job was to keep old crocks like her alive. Doctors

150

weren't "into death" as people put it nowadays. Behind her the young doctor tapped and prodded and listened.

"So how do you like it up at the Manor, Miss Ormsby?" he asked. "Nice place, eh?"

"Yes. It's very nice." How she loathed that word! Nice! What did it mean?

"You'll make friends," said Dr. Carswell, sitting down and writing on a prescription pad. "You'll have a good time up there," he added.

After a moment he told her that she could get dressed. He tore a sheet off the pad and handed it to her. "This is for more of your medication. Now don't neglect it. It's very important."

This amiable scolding was accompanied by a grin. He had, Miss Ormsby thought, a benevolent face and an heroic head.

"And cheer up, Miss Ormsby," he said. "Forget all this nonsense about death." Miss Ormsby looked across the room at an eye chart on the wall. She could still make out the letters on the top rows. That wasn't too bad. But she felt as she had so many times after so many classes. The point, it seems, had been missed entirely.

THIRTEEN

Mrs. Lucas sat at the card table wrapping the Christmas gifts that had arrived in the mail from the *Call of Tomorrow* people in California. She had ordered these items in July, and they were supposed to have arrived weeks ago, but that was the Post Office for you. You could hardly expect better nowadays. The sofa cushion would have to be mailed to Joan after Christmas, and Mrs. Lucas had already decided that she would ask Irma to look after that for her. The sofa cushion was not as large as the advertising literature had led her to believe; still it was very nice with the Lord's Prayer in gold lettering. On the other side was a drawing of the apostles in a boat on what she imagined was the Sea of Galilee. *Follow me and I will make you fishers of men.*

Mrs. Lucas put the cushion aside and examined her other presents for the family. The calendar would look very nice in Irma's kitchen next to the refrigerator. There was a Biblical saying and a message of inspiration from Pastor Bob for every day of the year. Mrs. Lucas had bought a calendar for herself as well. The plastic bookmarks with their passages of Scripture were for the children; they could use them in their school books. Goodness knows there was little enough religion in their

home, and these reminders might start the children thinking about their eventual destinations. Mrs. Lucas felt
proud of herself; she would have everything wrapped and
ready when Ward came by the next day to pick her up for
the holidays.

Mrs. Lucas vowed to herself that over the next few days
she would help Irma in every way possible. There were
any number of things she could do in that house: she
could dust the furniture and make the beds; she could
clean the bathroom, which, although Irma was a good
housekeeper, always looked as though it needed tending.
Mrs. Lucas had never been much of a baker, but there was
no earthly reason why she couldn't prepare the dressing
for the turkey. There was plenty she could do in that
house.

She could now hear Lorne Truscott's door slam. At the
card table Mrs. Lucas sat tensely, her head cocked to one
side, as alert and wary as a bird near a cat. Truscott was
singing some profanity and bumping into things. The old
fool had been into the liquor all day and was now stum-
bling about his own quarters. It was a disgrace the way
he'd carried on at lunch in the dining hall. And were the
nurses prepared to do anything about it? You may depend
they weren't. Why they just laughed! "Christmas!" they
said. "It's Christmas, Mrs. Lucas." But was the Lord's
birthday intended to be an occasion for drunkenness and
riot? It was shameful, nor would Mrs. Lucas have put it
passed the nurses themselves to have taken drink today.
She thought she could smell it on Nurse Fox's breath. As
she listened to Truscott's toilet flushing, Mrs. Lucas's eye
fell upon a verse from Exodus in the *Call of Tomorrow*
calendar. "Thy right hand O Lord is become glorious in
power, thy right hand O Lord, hath dashed in pieces the
enemy."

It was a torment to consider, but the fact remained that
old Truscott seemed to be thriving on the seeds. At such
times Mrs. Lucas was moved to wonder about the state of

cosmic justice and what indeed lay in store for her. Whither was she bound? It was a pity, but there was no one around anymore who could read the leaves. In the old days she and Dorothy Potter used to visit Madam Ramona, who would read the leaves to them. Mrs. Lucas hadn't thought of her friend Dorothy Potter in ages. Of course she was dead and gone now. Had been for years. Some said Dorothy was fast and it was true in a way; certainly she had her faults, as who hasn't? She could make you laugh though when she came into the kitchen with her cigarette machine and her copy of *Flash*. All those stories about the goings-on of rich men and their call girls in Toronto. Dorothy claimed to know about such things. She sat at the kitchen table and made her cigarettes, rolling the tobacco into the machine. It produced one long white tube and then she used a razor blade to slice off her cigarettes. She packed these into a case that once belonged to her father who was some kind of travelling salesman. Dorothy would go on about the plays on the radio: *Big Sister, Pepper Young's Family, Ma Perkins*. Or she would talk about some story in the *Flash* paper.

While she talked, she liked to take out a cigarette and tap it against the case, which she said was solid silver though Mrs. Lucas doubted that. Silver-plated nickel was more likely. That was another thing about Dorothy; she was always giving herself airs. Always pretending to be better than folks in Moreton because she came from the city. Still she had a good heart. You couldn't take that away from her. She used to loan Mrs. Lucas books you couldn't get at the public library. *Tobacco Road* and *God's Little Acre* and books like that. There was never much in them in Mrs. Lucas's estimation, though she had enjoyed *Forever Amber*. That was a good story.

Two or three times a year Dorothy would suggest they visit Madam Ramona, who had rooms in the Royal Hotel at the foot of the main street near the dockyards. When

154

Mrs. Lucas thought of those visits to the Royal Hotel, it was always a winter afternoon during the war, and she and Dorothy were climbing the wide bare steps to the second landing. The green radiators along the walls gave off a fierce heat and she always felt stifled in her mouton coat and galoshes. Both women wore pillbox hats with little veils. The Royal Hotel was by then no longer quite respectable. Most of its rooms were empty or occupied by older men, lifelong bachelors who worked on the lake freighters in the summer. There was a beer parlour on the main floor, and as Mrs. Lucas and Dorothy Potter climbed to the second landing in their heavy winter coats, they could hear the sound of men talking and laughing. The sound travelled up the stairwell with them. Dorothy was brazen enough about these excursions, but Mrs. Lucas always felt a shiver of fear that was not entirely unpleasant. In all her days she had never once told George or the children about the Royal Hotel.

Madam Ramona was of foreign extraction. You could tell that by her accent and her dark colouring. Mrs. Lucas always thought the fortune teller was some kind of gypsy or maybe a Jewess. While they drank their tea, Madam Ramona and Dorothy Potter smoked cigarettes and talked about rich people in Toronto who lived in mansions and drove Packard motor cars. Mrs. Lucas sat looking around the somber cluttered apartment with its mohair sofa and harmonium. Along the walls were pictures of bearded men in dark suits and women in shawls. The place smelled faintly of spices Mrs. Lucas could not identify. Below the frosted outer window, the business of the main street went on as usual; Mrs. Lucas could see people wrapped up in their coats and scarves walking to and fro; she could hear the chains on the wheels of cars and delivery trucks. It seemed as though she and Dorothy Potter and Madam Ramona were dwelling in another world entirely.

When they finished their tea, Madam Ramona would read the leaves, tilting the cups and gazing within to see all manner of shapes portending things to come. There was a path foretelling a journey; here were leaves formed into a purse and that surely meant money, perhaps an inheritance. Were there relatives in the family close to death? This, alas, was an apothecary's mortar and pestle and that signified illness. It would not, however, be serious. Perhaps a bad grippe. As one could see, the figures were quite small.

Once Mrs. Lucas asked Madam Ramona if she could see a house in the cup. She and George were then renting on Blake Street, and they had to get out by the end of the month. With the war on, housing was scarce in Moreton. And yes, Madam Ramona saw a frame house near a larger building, perhaps a church or school. And a week or so later, didn't they find the house on Second Avenue?

At the card table Mrs. Lucas could no longer hear any singing or banging about from Truscott's room. Perhaps he had fallen asleep and was even now lying on the floor in his vomit. "The crown of pride, the drunkards Ephraim shall be trodden under feet." Along with the calendars and sofa cushion, the *Call of Tomorrow* people had sent numerous pamphlets, and Mrs. Lucas decided that she would pass some of these under her neighbour's door. As Pastor Bob often said, it was a blessing to acquaint others with the Lord's message. Mrs. Lucas knew that the school teacher was now out; she had heard her leave earlier in the afternoon. It would be the work of a minute to slip the literature under her door.

As Mrs. Lucas arose from her chair, a current of pain hurried along her side. She hoped her bowels wouldn't kick up too much of a fuss during the Christmas concert that evening. From the other side of the wall came a sudden and terrible clatter. It sounded as though someone had dropped an armload of pans into an empty bathtub.

Mrs. Lucas next heard the voice of Lorne Truscott raised in song.

> *Last Saturday night I got married*
> *Me and my wife settled down.*

She paused for breath. The pocket of air beneath her ribs beckoned for release. As the voice of her tormentor rose and fell in song, Mrs. Lucas felt at once chastened and subdued by the struggle to prevail. She felt, too, a vast and satisfying pity both for herself and for all suffering creatures under the sun.

The afternoon sky was gray. A southerly wind pushed massive clouds onward, and through them one could glimpse the sun as it rolled along like a great pale coin. The radio people had said colder by nightfall and more snow for Christmas. In the cemetery overlooking the bay Miss Ormsby walked among gravestones that were now stained with dampness from the sudden thaw. The bare limbs of the trees glistened darkly, and underfoot the snow was heavy with moisture. It was snowball weather, and on such days Miss Ormsby liked to remember an afternoon when she had delighted pupils on her way home from school. That day a snowball had hit her solidly on the back. But instead of ignoring it and hurrying on, she had placed herself behind a tree and fired snowball after snowball at the surprised youths. Passersby cheered and applauded, and soon she had allies who helped her rout the enemy. It was a small moment of victory that was often referred to years later at class reunions and graduations.

Now she stepped carefully among the graves. It wouldn't do to fall; there was no one around to help if she were to break something. She imagined that most would see Bayview Cemetery as a queer place to be on a winter afternoon. Yet she had always felt a peculiar peace here among the town's dead. The names on many of the stones belonged to people she had once known; here were tradesmen and neighbours and former pupils and colleagues, friends and family. All now returned to the silence of minerals.

Miss Ormsby turned to look across the snow at the dark gray water of Georgian Bay. The water was rough and flecked with whitecaps from the wind.

> *Full fathom five thy father lies*
> *Of his bones are coral made*
> *Those are pearls that were his eyes:*
> *Nothing of him that doth fade*
> *But doth suffer a sea-change*
> *Into something rich and strange*
> *Sea-nymphs hourly ring his knell.*

She had been re-reading *The Tempest* lately and passages from the play remained fresh in her mind. It was encouraging to be able to recall such lovely words, but other signs of her faltering memory were distressing.

This afternoon for instance. After leaving the doctor's office, she had been embarrassed in the music store. She had gone there to buy two or three cassettes for her Walkman. But at the cash register she was obliged to admit that she had no money. When the clerk suggested a credit card, Miss Ormsby had laughed nervously; she had never owned such an article. Yet she could have sworn under oath that there had been two twenty dollar bills in her purse. And so while others watched, she had played the role of the little old lady who forgot her money, emptying the contents of her handbag onto the counter. And all to no avail! The money simply wasn't there. Either she had spent it or mislaid it. Whatever the case, she had forgotten, and that was worrying. When you began to mislay money, you were in trouble.

She had always been so careful about money. For over thirty years she had managed things on her own. Sitting at the little cherrywood secretary in the front hall, she had kept her bankbooks and her receipts from the superannuation fund in order. Fearful of the ignominy of debt, she had, like her father, paid her bills within days of their arrival. The mild damp wind pressed against her face and tugged at her green tam. She had pulled the hat closer about her ears as she stood in front of her parents' headstone and read their names. It was all she could do at this time of the year. In the spring she planted flowers. Each Sunday she weeded them with a little rake and watered the earth, using the tin dipper that hung by a hook on the water barrel.

Her mother was now only a distant memory. When she thought of her mother at all, Miss Ormsby remembered only a gentle unassuming woman who liked to play Bach and Schubert on the piano and who endured her short life quietly and without complaint. She died in 1937 at the age of fifty-two. Her husband lived on with his only daughter for another eighteen years. Beneath the gray snow lay stone markers upon which were the words "Mother" and "Father." Next to them was room for Miss Ormsby. She had arranged everything with Lewis Crawford at Crawford, Murray, and Hines. She had mentioned this once to Doreen, who professed astonishment. "Dear Aunty Kay," she exclaimed. "Dwelling on such negative things! You are by yourself too much these days."

What nonsense! She wasn't dwelling on anything; she had merely taken care of necessary arrangements. When her time came, there would be order and simplicity. There would be no hurdy gurdy tunes or newspaper rhymes. It was all on file in Lewis Crawford's safe. Miss Ormsby pulled back the sleeve of her coat and looked at her watch.

It was growing late. Already the spare December light was fading. At the Manor the evening meal would soon be on the table. If she wanted something to eat, she had better be present, and she had two buses to catch.

Miss Ormsby, however, lingered among the rows of graves. If she still lived in her house, she could eat when she felt like it. Tonight, for example, she could settle down with a book and a drink or two; it might be nine o'clock before she would have a bowl of soup. Now, however, she had to eat on schedule with the old men and the widows. It was like being a child in a boarding school, she thought, as she stopped in front of a small gray stone.

Adelaide Letitia Bales
1912–1985
Gone but not Forgotten

No indeed! Who could forget poor Addie? They had been friends for forty years.

Addie came to Moreton in September of the year the war ended. It was just months after Allan left. In her first years, Addie taught not only English and History, but also physical training. P.T. it was called in those days. Addie had been a gymnast at university, and she taught the girls how to balance on the parallel bars and leap across the leather horse. In those days she was a short sturdy woman in black gymnasium skirt and bloomers. Her cropped hair had already turned gray by her thirties.

She was bossy and sarcastic and many found her impossible. Nor did she mellow with age. She knew her stuff in the classroom, but the pupils had unflattering names for her. Few measured up to her expectations. She had set a face of disapproval against the world and being around her took some getting used to. When they began to take summer holidays together early in the sixties, there was always something that provoked Addie's scorn. On coach trips this woman or that man was an imbecile or a perfect ass. The driver was a maniac and they would all perish in a fiery wreck down the mountain side. Miss Ormsby smoked and drank too much. And why did she have eggs for breakfast every day? Was she not aware of the dangers of cholesterol? All this delivered in a hotel dining room in Williamsburg or Banff or Amsterdam.

The weight of these constant reproaches was a burden and sooner or later Miss Ormsby would rebel. It was often over something petty. "So we have the caves then this morning?" Addie would say at the breakfast table, raising her coffee cup to her mouth as she studied the brochures, her glasses down on her nose.

"You go ahead," Miss Ormsby would say. "I'm going to take a walk around the town."

Addie would look up as though suddenly confronted by the most appalling example of stupidity on record. "But the caves are included in the tour. Our admission is paid for, Kay. Why would you want to walk around the town this morning when we have already paid to see the caves. We'll have a walk around the town this evening."

"I am walking around the town this morning, Addie."

"But that's so silly. And wasteful."

"Nevertheless, that is what I intend to do."

Addie's eyes, big as plums behind her glasses, would return to the brochures. "Suit yourself then."

"I intend to."

After such a scene they would be separated by a bitter silence that neither seemed capable of breaking. Addie would suddenly find either the imbecile or the perfect ass an acceptable companion on the bus. In the mornings they would dress without a word, and in the evenings, they would eat their meal in silence. At the end of the trip, each would take her bags from the bus and wordlessly share a taxi home. Sometimes these awkward periods lasted well into the school year until one day in the staff room when a comment would reunite them as friends.

It was all such stupidity and stubborn-mindedness, thought Miss Ormsby, searching in her handbag for the Walkman. Did it really matter whether she looked at caves or battlefields with Addie Bales, or walked by herself in whatever town they happened to be in? The end of life levels everything, and during those last few weeks, she could hardly bear to look at Addie's ruined face and wasted body. Under the bare trees Miss Ormsby attached the Walkman, retying her scarf and settling the tam on her head. She listened. A divertimento by W.A. Mozart. Graceful. Delicate. Balm of Gilead on this winter afternoon.

FOURTEEN

Mrs. Rawlings was called away from the Christmas concert by Nurse Haines, who told her that the police were at the door. On the makeshift stage that had been erected in the gymnasium by the maintenance people, Lorne Truscott was singing "I Saw Mommy Kissing Santa Claus." To promote the song's comic effect, Lorne had removed his teeth and dressed himself in long red underwear. His performance was drawing forth much laughter from the residents who were seated in rows of plastic chairs.

Mrs. Rawlings, however, had serious doubts about the act, and so was perturbed at being summoned by the nurse. Within Mr. Truscott's vicinity always lurked questionable taste. It was not past his doing to unbutton the trapdoor in the underwear and present himself to the audience. Clearly, however, the police at the door was a matter of graver moment. And so Mrs. Rawlings hurried from the gymnasium past the nurses who were leaning against the back wall by the entrance. They had folded their arms across their chests and were laughing at Lorne's performance. Their presence was perfectly harmless, but nevertheless irritating to Mrs. Rawlings. Nurse Haines had just delivered a message about the police at the door, and now here she was laughing with the others. Mrs. Rawlings felt as might the captain of a great ship travelling through the night; when all was said and done, she alone had the burden of command to bear. With this in mind, she moved quickly and forcefully along the lower hall, a figure that looked quite capable of battering down a door.

The policeman, hatless though still wearing his blue vinyl parka, stood by the entrance to Mrs. Rawlings's office. Behind him in a chair sat Mr. Wilkie, who looked frail and rather gallant in his overcoat. His white silk monogrammed scarf and gray astrakhan lay in his lap. He was also wearing his blue suit with a striped shirt and bow tie. Pellets of freezing rain were breaking against the windows in Mrs. Rawlings's office.

"My dear Mr. Wilkie," said Mrs. Rawlings, observing the terrible night as she advanced past the policeman to her desk. "This surpasses amazement. Whatever can be the matter?"

The policeman, young and bulky and moustached, said, "Constable Jennings, Ma'am. The old gentleman came into the station about an hour ago, and started saying some pretty strange things. We just thought it best to hear him out and then bring him back. He seems a little disorganized."

Settled behind her desk Mrs. Rawlings asked, "Strange things, Constable? What sort of strange things?"

The young policeman looked nonplussed. To spare the old fellow, he was waiting for Mrs. Rawlings to dismiss Mr. Wilkie so that the circumstances surrounding the latter's visit to the police station could be explained without injury to his feelings. Mrs. Rawlings, however, had no notion of dismissing Mr. Wilkie, and so the policeman's considerate intentions were a wasted gesture. He soon gathered as much and said, "The gentleman seems to think that all the men in this place are being poisoned." The policeman shrugged as if to apologize personally for conveying such lunacy. "He claims it's all part of a plot by women to take over the world."

"My word!" said Mrs. Rawlings, suppressing clumsy laughter with a kind of snorting sound. "Poisoning all the men! Wherever would you get such a preposterous notion you poor dear man?" Mrs. Rawlings smiled at Mr. Wilkie, who was looking away from her at the dark wet window wherein he could see his own image and that of his enemy. The sight of Cora Rawlings's face, large and menacing, was hateful to him. He would have enjoyed striking it with a heavy blunt object. And was there any sense in discussing the matter with her? Would she sit still and listen if evidence were procured and presented? You could wager otherwise and be assured of gain. He would have nothing to say to any of them. When you couldn't trust officers of the law to come to your aid, then things had indeed come to a pretty pass.

"Mr. Wilkie," said Mrs. Rawlings to the policeman, "has been a model resident for the last three years. I simply can't imagine what got into the poor man's head. And what a night to be out of doors! Perhaps you have taken a chill, Mr. Wilkie. I shall have Nurse Haines take your temperature."

Mr. Wilkie's long fingers stroked the gray nubbly fur of his winter hat. It felt like poodle hair. Ada once had a little gray poodle named Daisy. She was seventeen when she died. They said it was a remarkable age for the species. Mr. Wilkie refused to look at Mrs. Rawlings, offering her only his handsome profile.

"Have you had anything to eat this evening, you poor dear man?" she asked. "I shall ask the kitchen to fix you a plate of soup. Piping hot! The very thing for this weather!"

"No!" Mr. Wilkie cried suddenly, half-rising in his chair. He sat down again. "I've already eaten," he added quietly. "At the chicken restaurant."

"I see," said Mrs. Rawlings, smiling at the policeman.

Mr. Wilkie, she decided, had turned the corner. They went suddenly like this sometimes; one day, coherent and sound as money in a vault; the next day, goofy as spring ducks. She would put in a call and reserve a bed for him at the Chronic Care Centre. The way things were shaping up, there would be any number of changes in the new year.

There were cries and moaning in the night, and Mrs. Lucas dreamed of an intruder with a dark moustache who seemed bent on ravaging her. When she awakened about two o'clock, she heard voices in the hall and thought at once of fire. There was a fire in the building and within minutes she would be roasted alive or expire from smoke inhalation. She sniffed the air but could detect nothing. Yet there were voices in the hall and flashes of dark red scored her window.

Mrs. Lucas found her glasses and struggled to sit up on the edge of the bed. But this sudden movement was taxing and a spell of dizziness swept over her. She had not heard the alarm bells, and now the nurses had forgotten her. With her bare feet she sought the mules that she had placed by the bedside hours before. In her haste, however, Mrs. Lucas kicked one of them under the bed. It was gone and would take an eternity to find. One slipper, of course, was of no use whatsoever. Straining to hear the crackle of flames, Mrs. Lucas cried out, "What about me? You're forgetting me." Her voice was a mere croak in the night.

Holding onto the wall with one hand, she made her way towards the door. There was no time to change clothes. She would have to go as she was, barefoot and in her oldest nightdress. There were big holes in the back of this garment; she had meant to throw it out ages ago. If she survived the fire, people would see the disgraceful way she dressed herself for bed. Mrs. Lucas felt like beating her fists against the door to protest the terrible injustice of it all.

When she opened the door, however, she saw no evidence of fire. Two men in blue parkas were wheeling a stretcher out of Lorne Truscott's room, and Mrs. Lucas felt a surge of happiness and relief unsurpassed in recent memory. The place was not burning down, and old Truscott was leaving as a sick man. Could one hope for more? *The seeds had worked after all.* Nurse Haines was holding Truscott's hand as the men in the parkas pushed the stretcher along the hallway toward the elevator. Was Truscott dead, wondered Mrs. Lucas? But then Nurse Haines would not be holding on to the hand of a dead man.

Mrs. Lucas stood by her doorway looking down to the end of the hall where the men were now maneuvering the stretcher into the elevator. None of the other apartment doors was open; no one else, it seemed, had been awakened by the commotion. At her doorway Mrs. Lucas was beside herself with excitement and curiosity. She would not close an eye tonight. But what of that? *The seeds had worked.* Truscott was now on his way out and Mrs. Lucas's heart was brimful. She watched Nurse Haines come back down the hallway. "Now Mrs. Lucas," whispered the nurse, "back to bed with you. It's two o'clock in the morning. You can't neglect your beauty sleep."

Nurse Haines had a flippant way about her that Mrs. Lucas always found provoking. On more than one occasion Mrs. Lucas had mentioned this to Mrs. Rawlings, reminding the administrator that some residents would appreciate a more serious attitude from the nursing staff. Mrs. Rawlings had always assured her that she would take the matter under advisement, whatever that meant.

"What seems to be the trouble with Mr. Truscott?" asked Mrs. Lucas, realizing, as she spoke, that her teeth were still immersed in the glass of Polident on the bedside table. For this reason her question was couched in words that were mushy with sibilants. Nurse Haines, however, took no notice of this; she was used to the ways of old folks at various hours of the day and night. "You must have heard the poor old guy moaning and groaning. He was carrying on something awful. I found him sitting on the edge of the bathtub, all bent over with pain."

"Is that a fact?" asked Mrs. Lucas. This indeed was news to hearten the weary and discouraged. "Did he have a coronary thrombosis or something?" she asked.

"No," whispered the nurse. "From the sound of him, I'd say it's probably his prostate."

"What's that?" asked Mrs. Lucas feeling a pang of disappointment.

"When some men get on in years," said Nurse Haines, "they have trouble with this gland in their rear ends." The nurse leaned forward and lightly socked Mrs. Lucas's arm. "At least it's one thing we won't have to worry about, eh?"

Mrs. Lucas frowned at the young nurse. What on earth was she going on about with this talk of men's rear ends?

"Sometimes," the nurse continued, "the gland enlarges with age and an elderly man has trouble passing his water. That's what's happened to Mr. Truscott tonight. He can't pass his water."

"Is that so?" said Mrs. Lucas, trying to imagine what a man's rear end had to do with his ability or inability to pass water. In any event, the subject was preposterous and distasteful; she was only sorry that the mouse poison had not contributed to the man's illness.

"The poor old guy," said Nurse Haines. "And he looked so cute tonight up on the stage in that long red underwear."

Mrs. Lucas ignored that observation. "Is this a serious business then?" she asked.

"Oh I don't think so," said the nurse. "They'll relieve his pain at the hospital and make him comfortable. Then they'll probably remove his prostate. It's a common surgical procedure. Men can live without them. I'd bet Mr. Truscott will be back with us in no time at all."

"Is that so?" asked Mrs. Lucas.

"Sure. Don't you worry, Mrs. Lucas. You'll have your neighbour back in a couple of weeks. Now you just trot right back to bed, and get your forty winks like a good girl." With this, the nurse gently pushed Mrs. Lucas back into her room and closed the door.

Behind the closed door Mrs. Lucas made a hideous face and padded to the window to watch the men in parkas load Lorne Truscott into the ambulance. Its revolving roof light threw patches of red across the parking lot and against her window. It was now snowing lightly and Mrs. Lucas watched the ambulance leave with its patient. Good riddance to bad rubbish, as her mother used to say. Old sayings like that had the ring of truth about them and no mistake. Mrs. Lucas was too excited to sleep. She sat instead at the card table sipping fruit salts and browsing through the *Call of Tomorrow* calendar with its messages of inspiration from Pastor Bob. She read, however, with only half a mind on the good man's words; the other half was thinking about Lorne Truscott's forthcoming operation. It was like they said, and she'd heard it more than once; when you went under the knife, anything could happen.

FIFTEEN

Sunset manor was astir with anticipation on the morning of Christmas Eve. Within hours relatives would arrive to take some of the old folks home for the holidays. For those staying in residence, it was a special time too. Chapel for Shut-Ins was sending around a minister that evening to conduct a nondenominational service. Stockings would be hung on the Christmas tree in the dining hall. On the big day, of course, there would be a turkey dinner with all the trimmings.

It was a time for celebration. Ahead, like a long dark tunnel, lay January, a month that was dreaded by everyone. During the bleak and pitiless weeks ahead, the earth would be frozen under snow and the wind would pour down from the boreal forests. It would snow every other day and few residents would venture outdoors. Visitors would be scarce. Joints would ache without respite and colds in the chest would linger. Breath would grow stale from too much cough syrup and the dry, overheated air. There were always some residents who maintained that if you had to go (and sooner or later you obviously had to), then January was the month to pack it in.

On Christmas Eve morning, however, the air of the Manor was charged with promise and good will. At the tables in the dining hall residents passed milk jugs and cereal boxes without being asked. There was Christmas music on the loudspeakers, and although by now a few residents would have enjoyed putting an axe through the sound system, they adopted the philosophical position that "Jingle Bells" and "Silent Night" would not last much longer.

Mrs. Huddle and Mrs. Somers spooned up their corn-flakes with good appetite. While doing so, they discussed Lorne Truscott's fate. One story circulating had Lorne already operated on for cancer of the bowels. According to this account, the doctors had just taken one look and closed him up; apparently there was nothing they could do. Another story claimed that Lorne had already passed away on the operating table. Whatever the truth, both women agreed that it was a shame to go like that over the holidays.

Mrs. Rawlings walked among the tables patting shoulders and shaking hands, wishing one and all a Merry Christmas. She watched Nurse Fox help Mrs. Fenerty with her porridge oats. The old girl was now well past it; by all accounts she too should have been on the list for the Chronic Care Centre. But she was such a pet to the staff and really no bother. Next year she would celebrate her one hundredth birthday and they would have a party for her with a telegram of congratulations from the Prime Minister and the Queen of England. Mrs. Fenerty was a dear old thing. Edna Lucas, however, was another kettle of fish. She was a troublemaker of the first water, and Mrs. Rawlings had plans for her in the new year. It might require a ruse of some description, but it would have to be done. With Truscott and Wilkie also gone, that would leave three beds available, thought Mrs. Rawlings as she smiled and extended holiday greetings to Mrs. Lucas, who was dressed to leave in a mauve pants suit.

It was later in the morning and Mrs. Lucas sat in one of the orange chairs in the Sun Room waiting for her son and daughter-in-law. Next to the chair she had placed a shopping bag with her Christmas presents for the family and her overnight case. Her winter coat was hanging on a rack in the hallway. Mrs. Lucas was tired but happy. Truscott was gone, and without him, the Manor was not such a bad place to live. She looked around the empty Sun Room and was content. It was a cold bright day and sunlight poured through the windows.

Mrs. Lucas had not been anywhere for months. The last time Ward and Irma had taken her for a drive was early in October. They came for her on a Sunday; there was to be a picnic in the town park by the bay. The children came along too and the day was mild and sunny. Indian summer weather, her father used to call it. But Ward was in a bad mood. He had become awfully cranky in middle age, and Mrs. Lucas could sense that something was wrong the minute he arrived.

Ward placed her in the back seat of the station wagon with the children, and she watched him go around the car and climb in and slam the door. Certainly he was in a mood; they all were for that matter. It came to her that there had probably been a family quarrel. And there she was, put into the midst of it. She could tell that her son was furious by the thrust of his jaw. As a child Ward had set his jaw just so when thwarted. Mrs. Lucas had observed the same trait in her grandson.

As they left the parking lot, the station wagon was enveloped in a thick awkward silence, and Mrs. Lucas wondered whether she should tell her granddaughter, who was sixteen, a joke she'd read in the *Reader's Digest.* When Debbie was a little girl, she used to laugh at her grandmother's stories. Lately, however, she'd become as sober as peas. As for Brian, Mrs. Lucas had never been

172

able to get much of a rise out of him. He was now thirteen and spent most of his time (so she was given to understand) in his bedroom working on one of these computers. Glancing sideways at her granddaughter's stormy brow, Mrs. Lucas decided against telling the funny story, and looked instead out the window at the lawns and trees of the town. The change of scenery was refreshing to the spirit.

At the park, however, they were surprised in an unpleasant way by the arrival of several busloads of people from a local institution who were having an outing of their own. In the wide parking area these people descended from the buses and were herded into groups by cheerful young men and women in tee shirts and shorts with armbands on their sleeves. Down the metal steps of the buses came the misshapen and the confused to stand blinking in the sunlight. Some laughed quietly, while others chanted odd little mantras of their own devising. A frail-looking young man made strange gestures with his hands. From time to time he fluttered them before his face. Mrs. Lucas thought the young man's hands looked like large white butterflies. There were mongoloid teenagers and forgetful old men and women afflicted with Alzheimer's; there were the palsied who writhed and jerked about like large puppets. It was all rather unsettling. Ward and Irma unloaded the picnic things, taking out the plastic lawn chairs and the luncheon hamper. They tried to ignore the hubbub around them.

The Lucas family seemed to be surrounded by the bus people, and a monstrously fat girl in pedal pushers reached out to touch Mrs. Lucas's granddaughter by the arm. The girl shuddered, and one of the young men with an armband smiled at her. "It's okay," he said. "Marie won't hurt you. She's just being friendly. She likes to touch people."

Things, however, improved. The Lucas family found a

picnic table under a large tree away from the others. The park authorities had assigned an area for the group, and they were assembling across the way near the bandshell. Dozens of picnic tables had been placed together for their meal, and there were to be games and races, for the young men and women with armbands were measuring off distances and laying out cord for the finishing lines. Ward unfolded a lawn chair for his mother and Mrs. Lucas took her ease.

It was the last weekend of the year for the amusement park nearby, and Mrs. Lucas and her family could hear the cries and laughter from those aboard the Caterpillar and the ferris wheel. The music from the merry-go-round reminded Mrs. Lucas of her childhood. And Irma put up a good lunch. Credit where credit's due. They had salmon and egg salad sandwiches and homemade pickles. There was a small chocolate cake and fruit and iced tea. Ward promised the children rides on the bumper cars and everyone's mood brightened.

After they had tidied up, Ward and Irma asked Mrs. Lucas if she wanted to go along to watch the children in the bumper cars. But Mrs. Lucas had said no, she was fine just where she was under the tree. She didn't let on that the heavy lunch and the mild, soft air had left her drowsy. Nevertheless it was true; she could barely keep her eyes open to watch the other picnic. Over there people were competing in an egg and spoon race, an event Mrs. Lucas hadn't watched in seventy years. Ward and Irma promised not to be long, and through heavy eyelids Mrs. Lucas had watched her family leave.

A moment later she was asleep and just as quickly (or so it seemed) awake again. Not twenty feet away stood a young man. He was perhaps nineteen or twenty and was pointing a forefinger at some imaginary person whom he was obviously scolding in his own way. The young man reminded Mrs. Lucas of a neighbour's child of long ago.

Mrs. Foster's boy. What was his name? Lawrence! Yes! Lawrence Foster. He used to run away from home and hide in the box cars by the dockyard. He once took a little boy into one of the boxcars. In the end they had to put him away. Lawrence Foster! Dead now of course, and the mother as well.

Mrs. Lucas watched the young man and began to feel mildly alarmed. He seemed unaware of her presence, yet what if he should turn his attention to her and perform a lewd act. What if he should decide to assault her as Lawrence Foster was supposed to have done to that child? Mrs. Lucas's fears had begun to multiply on that October afternoon as she sat in the lawn chair listening to the merry-go-round music and watching the young man. An unpleasant thickness gathered in her chest and she began to fear for her heart. Ward and Irma were nowhere to be seen, and Mrs. Lucas imagined dying by herself in the lawn chair under the tree. After a moment she got to her feet and hurried away towards the amusement park.

There amid the noise of the machines and the cries of the riders Mrs. Lucas lost her way. She saw only the faces of strangers. It was hard to credit that there were now so many people in Moreton, and all of them unknown to her. Yet that was the way it was anymore; you walked down the main street and you didn't know a soul. Mrs. Lucas wanted to sit down and have a cup of tea, but there was a long line-up at the restaurant and the snack bars did not serve tea. All the benches and picnic tables were in use and nowadays it was a waste of breath to ask young people to give up their seat for someone older. Finally she had sat on the grass near the carousel. People passing by took no notice of her.

Ward was furious when he found her sitting on the grass near the carousel with her legs outstretched and her shoes off. But what was she to do? She had felt ready to drop and her feet were swollen. One day he would know what it was like to have swollen feet. But Ward's face was red with anger that day. He told her that she had embarrassed him by sitting on the grass in her stockinged feet. She looked, he said, like an old bag lady, whatever that meant. Mrs. Lucas had never heard of the term. She tried to explain about her fear of the young man who reminded her of Lawrence Foster, but Ward wouldn't listen. He had taken her arm and hurried her away through the crowd. He was out of patience with her and kept asking who was Lawrence Foster. But he should have remembered Lawrence Foster. The Fosters lived on the corner in the yellow house next to the Marlowes. Ward was always going on about her memory and yet his was often worse than her own. She had disliked Ward that afternoon. It was not a pleasant memory at all.

Now Mrs. Lucas stirred from her reverie to see her son and daughter-in-law standing in their winter coats. "Having a little nap were you, Mother?" asked Ward. He was wearing a new winter coat made of some checked material, and in Mrs. Lucas's estimation the garment did not suit him. It made him look too portly. Mrs. Lucas's daughter-in-law bent down to kiss her cheek. She smelled of the cold winter day. "Merry Christmas, Mother," said Irma Lucas.

The pair of them had been angry with her that day in the park and with no good reason. They had no idea what she had been through that afternoon and they weren't prepared to listen to her explanation. Now they helped her to her feet and walked with her to the coat rack in the hallway. Ward carried the overnight case and the shopping bag with her Christmas presents in it. Mrs. Lucas's daughter-in-law, a tall pale woman, was also wearing a new winter coat. It was bright green and made her look, Mrs. Lucas noted with satisfaction, like a large stalk of celery.

Beyond Mr. Wilkie's window the shopping plaza was thronged with people and automobiles. Mr. Wilkie was fairly certain that it wasn't yet Saturday, and so was puzzled by all the commotion in the air. He guessed perhaps that some holiday was at hand. Standing by the window he watched the automobiles as they turned into the shopping plaza from Transit Road. The snow under the sunlight and the bright wintry day recalled his childhood and sled rides down Dunnin's Hill.

He reminded himself, however, that there was a job of work to be done; there was little point in idle reminiscence when one's survival was uppermost. Returning at once to his chair he sat down. The letter he had been working on was folded into the puzzle book, but it was only a rough draft on lined paper. It would need extensive revision, but the entire day lay ahead of him. The door was locked against intruders and he now had crackers and cheese enough to last a fortnight. Mr. Wilkie applied himself to the letter.

Dear Prime Minister:
  As a taxpayer and citizen and long-standing supporter of your party, I appeal to your sense of justice and fair play . . .

In the wavering white light Lorne Truscott could see a woman's face above him. The woman was holding his hand. The light in the room was glaring and he closed his eyes against it. He felt ready to go to sleep again. Once in a game in Collingwood some son of a bitch cross-checked him across the back of the neck and he hit the ice and went out cold. When he came around, he had felt something like this. Now the woman was trying to speak to him, but her voice sounded hollow and distant; it could have been

177

coming from inside a wooden barrel. He could remember the big wooden barrels of nails in the yard at the Foundry fifty years ago. Someone once had his leg crushed by one of those barrels.

He could vaguely remember joking with the nurses and doctors when they had wheeled him into the operating room. Now he guessed it was over. They had opened him up and taken something out of his arse. He couldn't feel a thing right now, though he supposed that in time it would hurt like hell. Meantime it wasn't so bad lying there. Lorne swore softly while the nurse squeezed his hand.

SIXTEEN

Nurse Haines opened the door to Mrs. Fenerty's room and shone the flashlight across the bed. The old woman looked like a mere bundle of clothes, and the nurse walked to the bed and stood listening. Sometimes the very old ones faded into death while sleeping. Nurse Haines bent across the bed and listened to Mrs. Fenerty's breathing. Then she left, closing the door softly behind her. After the nurse left, Mrs. Fenerty opened her eyes and lay staring into the darkness.

Sometimes she wondered where she was and why. Everything that mattered seemed to have happened so long ago. Her mother put ribbons in her hair when the days grew warm, and the big icicles hanging from the eaves of the house dripped and shrank and fell. Her father warned her not to stand under those icicles. The street smelled of horse dung and mud and she and Tommy played by the side of the house that was sheltered from the wind. Tommy pulled the ribbons from her hair and she cried and said she would tell Mother. So he gave back the ribbons and kissed her and made her promise not to tell. The next year, or the year after that, he took sick and died of the consumption. Poor dear Tommy, thought Mrs. Fenerty, staring into the darkness.

Miss Ormsby had settled into bed and was reading about the miraculous birth in the Gospel According to Luke. She preferred the sobering wisdom of Ecclesiastes, but it was Christmas Eve and her thoughts had turned to the event that inspired all the celebration, however degraded and foolish it had become. And there were many who still believed. She had been reminded of this by the pamphlets someone had slipped under her door.

And there were in the same country shepherds abiding in the fields keeping watch over their flocks by night.

And lo, the angel of the Lord came upon them, and the glory of the Lord shone round about them: and they were sore afraid.

And the angel said unto them, Fear not: for, behold, I bring you good tidings of great joy, which shall be to all people.

For unto you is born this day in the city of David a Saviour, which is Christ the Lord and this shall be a sign unto you; Ye shall find the babe wrapped in swaddling clothes, lying in a manger.

And suddenly there was with the angel a multitude of the heavenly host praising God and saying, Glory to God in the highest, and on earth peace, good will toward men.

Miss Ormsby put out her cigarette. On no account would she burn down the *facility*! She turned out the light, and swallowing the last of her drink, composed herself for sleep. Had the angels of the Lord foretold a miraculous birth in the hills of Palestine two thousand years ago? Did it really matter? The poetry was beautiful, and for that one was grateful. And like many things, the story itself was surely a cause for wonder. At the heart of all this life on earth lay mystery and wonder. In her bed Miss Ormsby lay waiting for sleep, wondering.